FIVE DOLLARS

HOW ONE ACT OF
KINDNESS CHANGED THE WORLD

CARL DOUGLASS
EVAN SWENSEN
KATHY HUGHES
JENNIFER RODRIGUEZ
MAGDEL ROETS
LOIS SWENSEN
REBECCA WETZLER
VALERIE WINANS

PUBLICATION
CONSULTANTS
We Believe In The Power Of Authors

8370 Eleusis Drive, Anchorage, Alaska 99502-4630
books@publicationconsultants.com—www.publicationconsultants.com

ISBN Number: 978-1-63747-401-3
eBook ISBN Number: 978-1-63747-402-0
Library of Congress Number: 2024942437

In a world where stories are often bound by solitary authorship, *Five Dollars: How One Act of Kindness Changed the World* breaks new ground. This book, as intriguing in its formation as in its content, is the collaborative masterpiece of a group of writers, each unaware of the others' identities or numbers. Each writer was tasked with weekly assignments and completed them within a solitary hour. Though born in isolation, these fragments were seamlessly interwoven by artificial intelligence, directed by human oversight, ensuring that the narrative remains a pure and authentic product of human creativity.

Manufactured in the United States of America

CONTENTS

CHAPTER ONE
THE UNRAVELING

Michael Zhang stood facing Jerry Bleven in Jerry's office where countless visions and projects had come to life. The walls, adorned with certificates of Jerry's achievements, stood as silent witnesses to his drive and the numerous times he had surged past expectations. This office, usually a beacon of activity and innovation, felt unsettlingly quiet today. Each framed accolade seemed to mock the sudden halt in Jerry's journey. His eyes, reflecting a clarity honed by years of navigating complex challenges, met Michael's—a man now grappling with the weight of unspoken words. Michael's usually steady demeanor was marred by a furrowed brow, revealing the internal conflict brewing within him.

"Jerry," Michael began, his tone more subdued than Jerry had ever heard. "Your contributions to this company have shaped what we've become. You've not just been an employee but a cornerstone. The board has made difficult decisions in light of our financial situation. We're facing cutbacks we hoped to avoid."

Michael took a deep breath, clasping his hands behind his back —a position Jerry recognized as his "bad news" stance. "Effective immediately, your position here is terminated. I'm sorry, Jerry."

"Terminated?" Jerry clasped and unclasped his hands as he absorbed Michael's words. Each syllable resonated with the finality of a eulogy rather than the progress reports they usually discussed.

"Michael," Jerry replied, his voice betraying a tremor he could not control. "But if you value my work so much, isn't there a way to keep me on? What about part-time? Consulting?"

Michael's face, usually an unreadable mask of executive control, softened, revealing a glimmer of regret. I've considered it from every angle a thousand times. The board is adamant. We're facing unprecedented times, Jerry. It's not a reflection of your work; it's reality biting back hard."

A pause hung in the air, filled with the unsaid. Jerry's mind raced with memories of late nights examining blueprints, early mornings spent in the office before anyone else arrived, and the sacrifices his family had made—dinners missed, school plays unattended, anniversaries postponed—all for the sake of a company now showing him the door.

"Reality..." Jerry echoed, the word hollow. "My reality is a mortgage, Michael. Kids who are looking forward to Christmas in a week. And I've been too busy to fix a car making a strange sound."

Michael stood up, moving to the window, his back to Jerry. "I remember when you came to us, fresh-faced, eager. You innovated the RX-2 systems when everyone else said it couldn't be done. You've been more than an asset; you've been a miracle worker."

The title Miracle Worker—one Jerry had earned for his knack for pulling off the impossible—now felt like an ill-fitting suit, a relic of better days. He took a deep breath, feeling the weight of a thousand moments pressing against his chest. "I'm sorry, Jerry. Truly, I am." Michael's voice was almost a whisper, blending with the distant hum of the city below. "I wish there was another way."

Jerry's gaze drifted to the photos on his desk—pictures of a smiling family, a graduation, a wedding—reminders of what was at stake. "We all have our responsibilities, Michael. I don't envy you this. But how am I supposed to tell Clara? The kids?"

A silence filled the space. Michael's gaze looked away, but in his eyes, a battle raged—one against the tide of a failing economy and the personal war he fought at home, where his wife's illness lay waiting, an unspoken shadow between them.

Finally, Jerry spoke, his words steady. "I always believed it would be enough if you worked hard and gave it your all. Seems I was wrong."

Pointing to the awards, certificates, and personal items around the office, Jerry asked, "What about all my things?"

"You can come by anytime to pick them up," Michael replied. "No need to worry about them now."

Michael turned, his eyes meeting Jerry's once more. "You weren't wrong, Jerry. The world is wrong."

With a final nod, Jerry turned and walked out of the office, the door closing behind him with a click, sounding suspiciously like a full stop. Jerry passed the cubicles, each a cell of focus and quiet determination, oblivious to the storm just breached his world. His colleagues, absorbed in their tasks, were shadows behind the flickering screens— shadows Jerry would soon join. He felt a sudden urge to speak, announce the injustice, and rally against the impersonal forces leading to his dismissal. But he swallowed the words. They were no balm for the wound he now bore; they offered no path forward. As he stepped into the elevator, he caught a reflection of himself in the polished metal doors—a reflection seeming to ask, "What now?" The answer was a chasm of uncertainty stretching before him. The ride down to the lobby was a descent in more ways than one.

Jerry's mind replayed the meeting with Michael, each word a sting, each moment of silence a suffocating pressure. He wondered about Michael's battles, the ones not fought in boardrooms but in private, where the cost of leadership weighed heavily on the heart.

The lobby doors opened to a blast of cold air, the city's winter breath. He wrapped his coat tight around him and stepped out into the crowd. The town was ablaze with Christmas lights, starkly contrasting with the cold now seeping into his bones. Jerry wandered, each step heavy with a dread he couldn't shake. The festive displays in the shop windows, the laughter and chatter of people around him, and the street vendors selling holiday trinkets seemed to belong to a different world now—a world where he still had a place, a role, a title.

A young couple brushed past him, holding hands and laughing, their shared joy a private language. He thought of Clara, her smile had always been his beacon, her resilience had been the bedrock of their family. How would he break the news to her? To their children?

His phone buzzed—a text from Clara, a simple heart emoji, and a question: "Coming home soon?" The message, usually a reminder of the warmth waiting for him, now felt like a herald of the cold he would have to bring into their home. Jerry tucked his phone away, his heart sinking. He wasn't ready to answer, not yet. He needed time to process, think, and armor himself for the impact this would have on their lives. And so, he walked, the city swallowing him, a man adrift.

The neon sign of the Quick Stop convenience store flickered in the gathering dusk, casting an electric glow onto the snow-dusted sidewalk. Jerry pushed through the door, the bell above it chiming a welcome, and felt strangely comforted in its normalcy.

The store was empty except for the clerk behind the counter, her tired eyes momentarily lighting up at the prospect of a customer. Evelyn Rodriguez had worked the late shift more times than she cared to count, the nights often blending in a parade of faces she barely remembered. But there was something about the man who now approached her, something in his stance showing defeat.

Jerry made his way to the counter, his footsteps slow, deliberate. He set down a quart of milk—a trivial purchase, yet it felt momentous, a mundane act in the face of his life's recent upheaval. He pulled out his old leather wallet, worn at the corners from years of use.

"Just the milk?" Evelyn asked, her voice hinting at the warmth she reserved for the few customers who seemed to need it.

"Yeah, just the milk," Jerry responded, attempting to smile. He handed her a twenty, his hands stilling as they brushed against the crispness of the bill. It was just a piece of paper, but it felt like the last vestige of his former life, a life where such a sum was inconsequential.

Evelyn returned his change, and their eyes met. "You look like you could use some good news," she said, half-joking yet sincere.

Jerry chuckled, a sound more exhale than mirth. "Good news? Haven't had any in a while."

"Tell you what," Evelyn said, leaning in like she was about to share a secret. "Why don't you take one of those scratch-off lottery tickets on the house? Who knows? Your luck might change."

Jerry paused, considering the offer. It was a kind gesture, a flicker of light on a day shadowed with darkness. He glanced at the display of colorful tickets, each promising fortunes just a scratch away. "No, I can't," he finally said. "But here, do something for me, would you?" He pushed a five-dollar bill he'd been holding toward her. "The next person who comes in, who looks like they need it... give them this. Maybe it'll change their luck."

Evelyn's expression softened, her usual reluctance giving way to surprise and something like respect. "Are you sure?" she asked. "People don't just give away money."

"I'm sure," Jerry insisted. "Call it a random act of kindness."

Evelyn took the bill, nodding slowly. "Okay, I will."

Jerry turned to leave, the bell chiming again as the cold air welcomed him back. He couldn't explain to himself why he had impulsively given five dollars away. It was not like him. What would he tell Clara?

Evelyn watched him go, the five-dollar bill in her hand. She knew the weight of every coin, the value of each dollar slipping through her fingers, each one a soldier in the battle she waged for her daughter's future. But as the door closed behind Jerry, she vowed to honor his wish and be the custodian of this small, hopeful deed.

———

CHAPTER TWO
THE EXCHANGE

Evelyn stood behind the counter at the Quick Stop, the brand-new five-dollar bill beneath the register. It was a quiet night making her feel like she was the last person awake. She glanced at the clock, the red digits crawling. Just a couple more hours, and she could head home to the tiny apartment she and her daughter called their corner of the universe.

The bell above the door jingled, pulling Evelyn from her reverie. A young woman stepped in, her coat thin against the winter chill, her eyes scanning the aisles with a hint of desperation.

Evelyn recognized the look—the calculation of needs versus means, a balancing act she knew all too well. "Evening," Evelyn greeted her, offering a smile she hoped would ease some of the woman's evident burden.

"Hi," the woman replied, her voice small. She picked a few essentials—bread, milk, a can of soup—and approached the counter, her countenance bracing for her choices' tally.

"That'll be $11.87," Evelyn said after ringing her up. She watched the woman's face fall as she fumbled with the ten one-dollar bills and tried to decide what to put back.

"You know what?" Evelyn said. "Someone left this earlier and told me to pass it on to someone who could use it." Evelyn slid the five-dollar bill across the counter.

The woman blinked, taken aback. "But... who just gives away money?"

"Someone passing through," Evelyn answered, echoing Jerry's words. "Consider it a random act of Christmas kindness."

Tears welled up in the woman's eyes as she accepted the money. "Thank you," she murmured, her gratitude filling the space between them. "This... this helps," she said as Evelyn told her to keep the five dollars; she'd make up the difference.

Evelyn watched her leave, the weight of the five-dollar bill lifted, not just from her hands but from her heart. As the night wore on, Evelyn's thoughts drifted to her daughter, asleep in her bed with dreams of Santa Claus dancing in her head. She thought about the bills, the classes she took to better their future, and the endless work cycle keeping them afloat. Evelyn made a mental note to share the story with her daughter in the morning; for every act of taking in this world, there could also be an act of giving.

When her shift finally ended, Evelyn locked up the Quick Stop and stepped out into the brisk air of the early morning. The city was quiet, the sky above just beginning to lighten with the promise of dawn. As she walked the few blocks home, her steps felt a little lighter, her spirit a touch brighter. And somewhere in the vast weave of the city, Jerry Bleven, without realizing it, had ignited a spark of hope carried forward by his simple, profound currency of compassion.

———

CHAPTER THREE
HOMECOMINGS AND HEARTSTRINGS

Jerry's hand hesitated on the doorknob of his home, the laughter and melodies of Christmas cheer spilling out from the cracks around the threshold. It was a threshold he now had to cross with the weight of his news, a weight threatening to tarnish the festive spirit within. He took a deep breath, mustering the strength o step into the light, heart, and warmth of his family.

The house was alive with the bustle of holiday preparations, the air rich with baked gingerbread and pine scents. Clara was the nucleus of this joyful chaos, her strawberry-blonde curls bouncing as she turned from the oven, her face lighting up at the sight of her husband.

"Jerry!" she exclaimed, her voice a melody above the Christmas tunes. "You're home early. Is everything—" Her words trailed off as she took in the sad set of his jaw, the uncharacteristic stoop of his shoulders. The children, too engrossed in their tinsel and tangle of lights, didn't notice the silent exchange between their parents.

Jerry managed a smile, though it didn't quite reach his eyes. "Hey, love," he said, closing the door behind him. "The house looks amazing."

Clara approached, her gray-green eyes searching his. "What's wrong?" she asked, a whisper meant only for him amidst the din of their home. Jerry admired her intuition; she always had a sense of the undercurrents of his heart.

Jerry took her hand, leading her away from the children, away from the joy, into the quiet sanctuary of their bedroom. There, amidst the familiar—their bed, the photo albums on the dresser, the faint scent of lavender—he told her.

"I was terminated today, Clara," he said, the words raw and jagged. "Financial downsizing—just before the holidays."

Clara's face was a canvas of emotions—shock, concern, and indomitable strength. She reached out, her touch a solace, her voice steady. "We'll get through this, Jerry. We always do."

Her resilience and unwavering support were a balm to his turbulent thoughts. "I know we will," Jerry replied, his hand finding the small of her back. "It's just... hard to swallow, you know?"

They stood together quietly, allowing the truth to settle around them. Then, slowly, Clara began to speak of practicalities, plans, and possibilities. Jerry shared his encounter at the Quick Stop, the five-dollar bill he'd passed on—an impulse now seeming both foolish and unnecessary.

Clara listened, her eyes glistening with unshed tears and something else—a pride in the man she married. "That's who you are, Jerry. You find a way to give even when the world takes from you." Their embrace was a silent vow, a promise to face the uncertainty together, to hold fast to the love and life they had built.

When they emerged from the bedroom, their faces were composed, their resolve like a shared armor. The children, oblivious to the storm their parents navigated, rushed to Jerry, their laughter a reminder of what truly mattered, of what remained unchanged in the shifting sands of circumstance.

Jerry knelt amongst them, swept into the simplicity of decorating a tree, hanging ornaments, and stringing lights. In those moments, surrounded by the innocence of his children and the strength of his wife, he found an anchor in the storm—a reminder, while he may have lost his job, he had not lost his purpose or the love making every challenge bearable.

As the Bleven family's evening drew on, the home's warmth stood in stark contrast to the cold reality lingering just beyond its walls. The children, immersed in the season's magic, wrapped themselves in the simple joy of holiday traditions, unaware of the complexities burdening their parents.

Jerry found himself amid a tug-of-war between the present merriment and the uncertainty of the future. He wove tales for his children of Christmases past, of grand family gatherings and laughter filling rooms, all the while knowing this year, the laughter would have to stretch a little further, and carry a little more weight.

Later, when the kids were tucked in bed, dreams of sugar plums dancing in their heads, Jerry and Clara settled into the quiet living room, the glow of the Christmas tree casting a soft light on their faces.

Clara broke the silence, her voice steady but soft. "We have some savings," she began. "We'll manage for a while. We can cut back on a few things..."

"But not Christmas, Clara. I won't have them remember this year as the time Dad couldn't make it happen," Jerry interjected, his words firm, resolute.

Clara nodded, her eyes meeting his. "We'll make it the best Christmas they've ever had," she said. "They won't feel a thing. This will be our gift to them—a bubble of happiness, no matter what."

They spoke of plans, adjustments, thriftiness, and the little luxuries they could forgo. But beyond the pragmatic discussions, there was an unspoken understanding they were not merely planning for a season but fortifying their family for the times to come.

Clara mentioned the five dollars Jerry had given away as they worked through their budget. "It's more than just a gesture, isn't it?" she mused. "It's a statement—a declaration you haven't lost who you are despite everything."

Jerry looked at her, his heart full. "When everything's stripped away, Clara, when the titles and the accolades don't mean a thing...when you find out what you're made of."

Clara reached out, her hand covering his. "And you, Jerry Bleven, are made of the strongest stuff. You always land on your feet."

As the night deepened and the embers in the fireplace glowed a little less brightly, Jerry and Clara remained side by side, partners not only in name but in the truest sense. They were each other's compass in the storm, a beacon for the other when the way seemed dark.

The following day, the house awoke to laughter and the aroma of fresh pancakes—a tradition Jerry insisted on keeping, even now. As they gathered around the breakfast table, the job loss and the financial troubles were unspoken shadows, kept at bay by the light of family and the power of resilience.

Jerry looked at each of his children and Clara and felt profound gratitude. They were why he'd work twice as hard to find a new path and keep smiling, encouraging, and loving, no matter what life threw his way. Ultimately, it was not the job defining him but the love he gave and the strength he drew from those he cherished. This understanding, this certainty, was his guiding star.

And so, with bellies full and hearts joined, the Bleven family faced the day—a day not promised to be easy but promised, nonetheless.

———

CHAPTER FOUR
THE DAWN OF RESOLVE

S andy Jones' steps echoed with determination as she ascended the stairs to her apartment, the five-dollar bill folded neatly in her wallet, lighting up the shadowy hallway with a glimmer of hope. Her mind raced with the potential and possibilities laying ahead. This job interview could pivot her life toward stability and away from the precarious edge on which she had balanced for far too long.

Opening the door, the sight greeting her doused her in a cold reality. There sat Jack, sprawled out on the sofa with a bottle dangling from his fingers, a picture of neglect. On the floor, her daughter Lilly played silently with her mess of curly hair and cherubic face, her innocence starkly contrasting the scene of despair.

"Lilly, baby, why are you not in bed?" Sandy asked, her voice a mixture of relief and reproach as she scooped her daughter into her arms.

"I waited for you, Mommy," Lilly's small voice held a note of sleepiness and reproach. "Daddy's funny," she whispered, her eyes wide with the wisdom of a child who has seen too much.

Jack's eyes flickered open, the glazed look sharpening as he focused on Sandy. "You're home early," he slurred, an attempt at casualness fooling no one.

"And smiling," she replied, masking the turmoil inside her. "Looks like you have good news?"

Jack's grin spread, unfurling a flag of false triumph in their meager living room. "I do, Sugar. I have something great to show you." He produced a necklace, dangling it before her eyes. The jewels glinted mockingly—a cruel reminder of the opportunities he'd squandered.

Sandy clenched her hands into fists at her sides, her heart thundering against her ribs. "Jack, where did this come from?" she demanded, her voice steady despite the rising anger.

His reluctance was palpable, but with Sandy's unwavering gaze drilling into him, Jack told her. "Phil spotted this nice house. The people are away on holiday. He watched them for some time and saw them leave with lots of luggage."

Sandy's mind reeled as Jack's admission sunk in. "So. You're no longer a petty thief but have taken the next step. You've become a burglar?" Her voice was low, but its fury and disappointment were unmistakable.

With purposeful strides, Sandy moved to their bedroom and tossed Jack's clothes into a duffel bag. The once shared space of intimacy and privacy was now a staging ground for separation.

"Hey, Sugar, what are you doing?" Jack's voice, now laced with confusion and a hint of fear, followed her.

"Throwing you out," she said, her words slicing through the tension. "Last time I told you, if you steal anything ever again, you're out. And this time, you've overstepped big time. I cannot, and I will not live like this."

Jack stood, his movements clumsy, inebriation muddling his coordination. "You can't do this to me, Sugar; you need me," he pleaded.

"I need a man I can depend on. Not a thief, too lazy to work. Now go."

His objections were met with deaf ears. Sandy was resolute. The line had been crossed, and there was no turning back.

"Where will I go this time of night?" Jack's voice cracked, and the vulnerability he so often masked with bravado made a rare appearance.

"Ask your buddies. I'm sure they will love to take you in," she retorted, her resolve hardening against his pleas.

Sandy's hands shook as she handed him the bag, a tangible symbol of her decision's finality. Jack's exit was met with the click of the lock sliding into place, a sound reverberating with the closing of a chapter in Sandy's life.

Returning to the kitchen, she poured herself a cup of coffee, the bitterness on her tongue a stark contrast to the sweetness of Lilly's sleepy embrace. Taking the five-dollar bill out of her purse, she whispered a prayer of gratitude and resolve, thanking a higher power for preventing her from making a mistake at the Quick Stop and giving her the strength to end the cycle of deceit trapping her family.

Sandy's neighbor, Mrs. Greta Olsen, had been listening through the thin walls, her heart aching for the young woman she'd watched struggle and persevere. When Sandy's resolve cracked the silence of the apartment complex, Greta knew it was time to act. As she crossed the threshold into Sandy's apartment, she saw the aftermath of Sandy's resolve, Jack's absence a void filled with potential. She noticed the money in Sandy's hand and said, "I'll watch Lilly when you work. I'll do it without pay while you get on your feet.

Sandy's eyes met Greta's, a torrent of emotions swirling within. "You would do this for me?"

"For you and Lilly," Greta affirmed, her voice unwavering. "We'll talk tomorrow," she said as she closed the door and left.

Sandy stood momentarily when a knock sounded at the door—a harbinger of another twist in Sandy's ever-complicating life. It was Jack, his face bruised, his eyes desperate. He had been robbed by the same 'buddies' he had committed the burglary with.

Sandy faced him, not with the anger of before but with a newfound pity and detachment. "You have to go, Jack," she said, her voice steady. "And this time, for good."

Jack's gaze lingered on Lilly, the daughter he hardly knew, and Sandy saw the flicker of what could have been—a loving father and a supportive husband. But the flicker died as quickly as it came, extinguished by years of disappointment.

Holding the bill between her fingers, Sandy turned to face Jack, his image contrasting the life she was rebuilding. Clouded with regret, his eyes met hers.

"Take this, Jack," she said, the five-dollar bill extending toward him, her gesture deliberate. "I want you to know how I got this bill. It was given to me by someone who didn't know me when I felt the world had nothing left to offer. Things have started to change since this bill came into my life." Her eyes met Jack's, asking him to understand the importance of the small piece of currency.

"Jack, I need you to leave—for good. But I hope you remember what it meant to me when you look at this bill." Jack looked at the bill and then back at Sandy, not fully understanding what giving up the five-dollar bill meant to her.

As the door closed behind Jack, she turned to Lilly, who stood with her favorite stuffed bear clutched tightly against her chest. Her eyes were wide with a mix of confusion and relief.

Sandy knelt to meet Lilly's gaze, her own eyes softening. "Sweetheart, things will be different from now on, but no matter what, I want you to know we're going to be okay."

"Is Daddy coming back?"

"No, my love. It's just going to be you and me now. And Mrs. Olsen is going to help us out a little too."

Then, she smiled in the earnest manner of children who quickly adapt. "Can we have pancakes for breakfast now?"

———

CHAPTER FIVE
UNSEEN THREADS

As Evelyn's footsteps echoed softly down the quiet corridor of her apartment building, the smell of old wood and fading wallpaper lingered in the air, a comforting yet poignant reminder of the countless evenings she had returned home with the weight of the day behind her. A different kind of anticipation stirred within her tonight as she approached the familiar door.

With a gentle click, the lock released, and Evelyn stepped into the apartment she and her daughter, Amy, called home. Their modest living space, bathed in the soft glow of a streetlamp filtering through gauzy curtains, seemed to welcome her with an air of expectant quiet.

Setting down her keys, Evelyn's mind replayed the night's tender episode—a simple act of kindness at the store feeling like a beacon in the monotony of her daily grind. It had sparked something, a flicker of possibility, the idea that significant change could begin even in their small world.

Inside, curled up on the couch under a mound of blankets, Amy pretended to read, but her alert and scanning eyes betrayed her anticipation for her mother's return.

"Mom, how was work?" Amy's soft voice filled the room, her words weaving warmth into the cool air.

"It was more than just work tonight," Evelyn replied, her tone imbued with a hint of mystery as she draped her coat over a chair and joined Amy on the couch. "Something happened—something good."

Intrigued, Amy shifted to make room, her book forgotten. "Tell me," she urged, her eyes wide with curiosity.

Evelyn wrapped them both in the blanket, pulling Amy close. "There was a woman who could barely afford her groceries... " Evelyn paused, ensuring she had her daughter's full attention. "Someone had left a five-dollar bill with instructions to pass it on to someone in need. So, I did."

Amy's eyes sparkled with the unfolding story, the gears of her young mind already turning. "And then? What did she do?"

"She was so thankful, Amy. It turned her whole night around. Maybe more than just her night." Evelyn's voice was thoughtful, her mind weaving through the possibilities. "It made me think—what if we started doing things like that? Small things to help others?"

"Like a kindness mission?" Amy suggested.

"Yes, exactly! But with our twist. We could create a chain reaction of goodwill right here in our neighborhood."

Amy whispered with playful seriousness in her tone. "We become agents of change, secret kindness agents."

Evelyn laughed, a genuine, hearty sound chasing away the last remnants of her fatigue. "Agents of kindness, then. Let's start with what we have, and who knows how far it can go?"

Just as they were sketching out their grand plans, the harsh reality intruded in the form of a phone call from a distressed neighbor needing help. With a rueful glance at Amy, Evelyn excused herself, her sense of duty pulling her away from their dream.

Evelyn hurried to assist her neighbor, her mind racing with thoughts of leaky pipes and water damage and flickering back to the plans she and Amy were hatching. They were going to need to be adaptable and resilient. She knew life didn't always wait for one's plans to be convenient.

The crisis was managed, and her neighbor was reassured; Evelyn returned to their apartment, her spirit undampened. She found Amy still awake, the makeshift plans they'd started scattered around her on the coffee table like puzzle pieces.

"We had to pause our plan, but we're back now and ready to keep going. This—helping our neighbor—was the first step. Real kindness doesn't wait for the right moment."

Amy nodded, inspired by her mother's words. "So, what's next?"

"We start small. We use some of our savings tomorrow to buy groceries for Mrs. Jackson next door. She's always struggling to make ends meet at the end of the month," Evelyn suggested, her eyes alight with the prospect of their secret mission.

The reality of their financial limitations crept in, dampening their enthusiasm. Evelyn saw the concern in Amy's eyes and took her hand, squeezing it gently. "We'll make it work. Kindness doesn't have to be big to be impactful. It's the thought and the effort that count."

The following day, Evelyn and Amy set about implementing their plan. They pooled together their little extra and bought essential items for Mrs. Jackson. Their excitement was palpable as they secretly placed the bag by her door, a note tucked inside promising anonymous support and hope.

Amy said, her voice tinged with pride as they watched from their window, Mrs. Jackson discovering the surprise. "We did it, Mom. We really helped someone!"

"And this is just the beginning," Evelyn assured her, envisioning a future where these small acts of kindness would weave a new fabric into their lives.

Amy's enthusiastic planning and Evelyn's willingness to engage sparked interest among their neighbors. Word of their deeds spread, not through grand announcements, but through the quiet network of shared glances and whispered stories, igniting a communal desire to participate.

As they sat together, Evelyn felt a profound sense of connection. Their little project, born from a simple act of kindness at a convenience store, was growing, weaving new patterns into the fabric of their lives and their community.

———

CHAPTER SIX
THE FIVE-DOLLAR REDEMPTION

In the afterglow of the muted Christmas lights, Jerry sat at his worn wooden desk that had witnessed his many triumphs. Now, it felt like an altar for a different kind of offering—his future. The soft glow of the laptop was a lighthouse in the fog of his thoughts as he pondered his next move.

The usual cheer of the holiday season had taken on a different hue in the Bleven household this year. The walls, adorned with frames capturing echoes of laughter and milestones, now seemed to look on with sad patience. The air was thick with silence speaking volumes, punctuated by the soft tapping of Jerry's fingers on the keys.

A series of numbers—a calculation of savings against expenses, a subtraction leaving little room for denial. Yet, amid these calculations, Jerry's mind drifted back to the five-dollar bill he'd handed to the Quick Stop clerk. It was a small act, but it was something.

A gentle knock at the door broke his concentration as Jerry navigated the sea of job listings. It was Clara, her eyes carrying the weight of concern and the unspoken fear of the future. "Any luck?" she asked, her voice a tender thread in the fabric of his resolve.

"Not yet," Jerry replied, his gaze not leaving the screen. "But there's something... freeing about starting anew. Maybe this is a chance to find something more fulfilling."

Clara moved closer, her presence a warmth against the chill of uncertainty. "We'll get through this," she said, her hand finding his, "together."

The fabric of the Bleven family was being tested; each thread was pulled taut by the strain of change. Yet, in the strength of their unity, a new pattern was emerging—a design they had yet to understand but one they were crafting with each shared moment of fortitude.

Inspired by Clara's unwavering support, Jerry allowed himself a moment of reverie. There, in the sanctuary of his home office, he envisioned untraveled paths. A memory surfaced: a conversation with an old friend who had reinvented his life.

The phone rang, slicing through the quiet contemplation. It was the same friend, Mark, calling with a timeliness bordering on serendipity. "Jerry, I heard about losing your job. I've been there, remember? Let's meet up—I might have something you may be interested in."

Their meeting was arranged for the next day, a rendezvous at a quaint café holding memories of their youthful ambitions.

Jerry stood before his closet the next day, deliberating on what to wear for the day's journey. Clara entered the room, her eyes alight with curiosity and concern. "You look fabulous. Where are you going, Jerry?" she inquired.

"I'm off to see Mark and a couple of guys, see if any of them know about an opening somewhere," Jerry replied, his tone tinged with hope and uncertainty.

Clara smiled. "That's great, honey. Keep going. I'm certain you'll find a good job soon."

"You are such an inspiration to me," Jerry remarked, his voice filled with admiration. "When I'm down, you always pick me up with your positive attitude and enthusiasm."

"It's because I believe in you. Now, go and find your dream job. But do me a favor. I am too busy to run to the store but need a few items. Would you mind getting them for me on your way home?" Jerry nodded in agreement with Clara, his determination to succeed burning brighter than ever.

Jerry set out with Clara's list in hand, his mind buzzing with possibilities. He parked his car in a central location, ready to embark on his quest for a new beginning.

As he entered the cozy café where they agreed to meet, Jerry's eyes scanned the room, searching for his old friend. And there, seated at a corner table bathed in warm lamp-light, was Mark, a smile spreading across his face as he caught sight of Jerry.

"Jerry, my man!" Mark greeted him, rising from his seat to embrace him in a bear hug. "It's been too long."

The two friends settled into their seats and exchanged life updates since their last encounter. Mark's easygoing demeanor and infectious enthusiasm lifted Jerry's spirits, infusing him with optimism he hadn't felt in weeks.

"So, tell me about this job you mentioned," Jerry prompted, leaning forward with anticipation.

Mark's eyes twinkled with excitement as he launched into an animated description of a startup he had recently joined. "It's a game-changer, Jerry. We're disrupting the industry in ways you wouldn't believe. And the best part? We're looking for someone just like you to join the team."

As Mark outlined the role and its growth potential, Jerry felt a sense of excitement bubbling within him. Here was an opportunity to break free from the confines of his past and embrace a future filled with possibility.

Just as Jerry was about to commit to the opportunity, his phone buzzed with a series of missed calls and voice-mails. With a furrowed brow, he glanced at the screen, his heart sinking as he saw the familiar names of other contacts he had planned to contact.

"Sorry, Mark. I need to take this," Jerry apologized, rising from his seat with a sense of unease. As he stepped outside to return the calls, a nagging doubt crept into his mind, whispering of missed opportunities and uncertain futures.

Returning to the café, Jerry approached Mark. "I'm not able to commit right now, Mark. Can you give me some time to think about it?"

"Of course, Jerry. Take your time."

And as they shook hands and departed, Jerry promised to return to Mark in a few days.

His next call was with Andy Grovner, his old friend from college. "Hey, Jerry, good to see you," Andy's familiar voice greeted him as he entered Andy's plush office. After exchanging pleasantries, Jerry shared the details of his job loss and the purpose of his visit.

Andy listened intently, offering words of encouragement and a promise to keep an ear to the ground for any possible opportunities, but nothing more.

At his next stop, Jerry met Gary, a distant cousin of Clara's, who offered leads on potential job openings. Armed with two business cards and a glimmer of optimism, Jerry moved on.

As he made his way to his car, his thoughts swirled with anticipation and trepidation. Jerry couldn't shake the nagging feeling Mark's offer might not suit him.

Deep in thought, he navigated the familiar streets toward home, his mind consumed with the weight of his uncertain future. As he idled at a traffic light, a sudden realization struck him: Clara's list. He had completely forgotten about it."

With a muttered curse, he made a split-second decision, veering off course toward the nearest convenience store. As he entered the store, the familiar chime of the bell above the door greeted him, accompanied by the soft hum of fluorescent lights.

To his surprise, the cashier behind the counter greeted him with a warm smile, her tired eyes twinkling with kindness. It was the same woman to whom he had given a five-dollar bill just weeks before, a small act of kindness born from his own struggles.

"How are you today, sir?" Evelyn's voice was gentle, and her smile was genuine.

"Very well, thank you," Jerry replied. "Last time I was here, I had just lost my job, but I might have found something today. How about you?"

Before Evelyn could respond and tell Jerry about giving a customer his five dollar bill and what she and her daughter had been doing, a man came around the shelves from the back of the store, his expression curious. As Evelyn explained Jerry's situation, the man's eyes lit up with interest.

"So, you're job hunting. What do you do?" the man asked, his tone businesslike yet curious.

Jerry explained his background and qualifications. The man listened intently, nodding along as Jerry spoke.

Handing Jerry a business card, the man offered a small smile. "One of the big managers in the company died of a heart attack last week. I doubt if there is anyone experienced enough to fill the job. Give this guy a call and see what happens."

Jerry pocketed the business card, thanked the man, and gathered up the items on Clara's list. As she finished checking Jerry out Evelyn started to tell him how his generosity had impressed her and her daughter and about giving his five dollar bill to a woman a customer interrupted her with questions, and before she finished answering, Jerry had left the store.

As he left the store with Clara's items in hand, a sense of gratitude welled up within him for the unexpected twists and turns bringing him to this moment. There was always the promise of new beginnings amid uncertainty, waiting to be embraced with open arms.

With the weight of Clara's errands lifted and a newfound sense of purpose guiding his steps, Jerry returned home, his heart light with anticipation for the future ahead.

As he entered their cozy living room, Clara greeted him with a warm smile, her eyes shining with pride.

"Did you manage to get everything?" she asked, her curiosity tinged with amusement.

Jerry grinned, holding up the bag of items. "Mission accomplished," he declared triumphantly, a sense of satisfaction coursing through him.

Clara laughed, shaking her head in mock disbelief. "I never doubted you for a second."

As they settled into their evening routine, Jerry was left in awe by the day's incredible and unforeseen events. From Mark's timely call to the chance encounter at the convenience store, every twist and turn seemed to lead him closer to his destiny.

A sense of peace settled in as he drifted off to sleep. His dreams were filled with visions of the bright future lying ahead. For in the fabric of life, each thread was woven with purpose, guiding him ever closer to his dreams.

———

CHAPTER SEVEN
ECHOES OF ALHAMBRA

Echoes of Alhambra's fountains, once a symphony coursing through Maria Innocenta Garcia's dreams, had faded by the time the morning sun cast its first glow on her bedside table. Her sleep, crowded with visions of youth and play, dissipated into the solemn stillness of her spacious, artifact-laden bedroom. There, enveloped in sheets whispering of forgotten threads of joy, the weight of ninety-four years lay upon her—the repercussions of a full life now quieted by the hush of solitude.

Maria's morning began, as it had for countless days before, with an inventory of aches and a body's slow, deliberate motions bearing the marks of time. The mirrors, unforgiving in their truth, reflected a figure carved from life's relentless passage—a woman who had danced at balls, raised children, and outlived some of her children. The quiet hum of her grand estate did little to fill the void of laughter long since migrated to the corners of her memory.

As she steadied herself against the rich mahogany of her staircase, her gaze fell upon a peculiar sight—an envelope trespassing into her isolation, its edges just peeping from under the grand front door. With a mixture of curiosity and the remnants of her dream still clinging to her thoughts, Maria reached for the envelope using the grasping tool that had become her intermediary to a world seeming to shrink with each passing day.

Inside, a five-dollar bill—a crisp, unassuming resident of the paper sleeve—lay against a note. "Dear Maria," it read, "this is a gift that keeps giving. Enjoy your day and your life. Pass it on and make someone else happy." The words, kind and cryptic, were a splash of color on the canvas of her monochrome routine.

A fire, long dormant, began to crackle within Maria. Wealth had been her companion for decades, a silent partner to her philanthropy and indulgences. But this simple gesture, this note, and its modest companion stirred a sense of purpose money alone had never achieved. It was as if the five dollars carried the vitality of her Alhambra, the children's laughter, and the warmth of human connection had become rare in her gilded cage of old age.

Maria did not simply pocket the bill or place it on her mantel as a memento. No, it served as a catalyst, sparking an idea shimmering with the potential to crack the veneer of her solitary existence. With each creak of her joints, she maneuvered through her morning with a determination belied her frailty, a plan unfolding with each step toward the telephone.

With the telephone receiver pressed gently to her ear, Maria's voice, a rich tone seasoned by time, requested a connection to Mary Elena, her confidante within the marbled halls of the bank. She awaited the familiar click and the soft purr of the line ushering in a voice from the outside world, a thread still tieing her to the means of society and commerce.

"There's something I need you to do for me, Mary Elena," Maria spoke with an inflection dancing between command and caprice, a tone cultivated from years of being both a patron and a friend. "I would like to make a very particular withdrawal. In fives, if you please. Crisp and unused—there's a certain charm to them, don't you think?"

As the hum of acknowledgment buzzed through the line, Maria turned to face the day with a newfound purpose. She navigated the expanse of her bedroom, each step a defiance of the pain clinging to her bones, each movement a little smoother, a little more determined than the last.

Her fingers, gnarled and beautiful, betrayed her with their stiffness as she set about her task. Still, they were the same fingers she had penned love letters, dried tears, and clung to her beloved Leopold in a dance lasting decades. Now, they would orchestrate a different kind of waltz—a dance of giving extending beyond the polished floors of her estate.

Maria began stationed at her writing desk, a relic of oak and history. She pulled from its drawers the stationery that had slept undisturbed for seasons, its texture still eager to drink in ink and intentions. Once a mere accessory to her thoughtful moments, the pen became the conduit for a cascade of kindness she was about to release.

With each note written, Maria infused her script with the warmth she had received from the anonymous five-dollar gift. She imagined the faces of old friends, the laughter of children now grown, and the surprise of strangers as they encountered her small tokens of joy. This was her orchestra now, the scratch of pen on paper, the music filling her home with echoes of purpose.

The labor of love was not without its cost. Fatigue draped itself upon Maria like a shawl, and her eyes, once sharp as a falcon, now grew weary with the effort of her endeavor. Rest beckoned, and she heeded its call, allowing herself moments of reprieve where dreams of Alhambra's gardens once again played behind her closed lids.

The list of names before her—a roll call of lives intersecting with her own—grew shorter with each envelope sealed. It was a litany of her past, each name a story, each story a thread in the fabric of her life. As she affixed stamps to each letter, Maria felt the years fall away, her spirit invigorated by giving.

The evening approached, the sky a canvas of purples and oranges blending into the horizon. Maria's mission, a day's worth of intention and memory, sat in a stack on her desk. It was an army of envelopes, each a bearer of potential change, each a testament to the power of a single, thoughtful act.

As Maria contemplated the fruits of her labor, she felt a connection to the world she had not felt in years. It was as if the walls of her estate had expanded, embracing the city, the country, and the globe itself. With all its chaos and beauty, the world didn't seem so distant anymore.

As twilight melded into the inky embrace of night, Maria rested in her high-backed chair, her silhouette framed by the soft lamplight turning her room into a tableau of gentle shadows. The envelopes lay before her, each one a promise, a whisper of kinship soon to be dispatched into the world's great expanse.

The following morning, Maria rang for her neighbor's daughter, Sofia, a sprite of a girl with a heart as open as the sky. Sofia, with her youthful exuberance and boundless curiosity, had often assisted Maria, finding solace and wisdom in the stories Maria wove from her past. "Take these," Maria said, her voice imbued with conspiratorial glee, "and ensure they find their way to the hands of the postmaster. They are my soldiers of joy, and today, they march forth."

Sofia accepted the envelopes, and her journey to the post office became a mission, with each step purposeful and each breath a silent vow to honor Maria's trust. The envelopes, once confined to Maria's estate, were now emissaries venturing into realms anew.

As each envelope began its journey, propelled by the intricate dance of logistics and fate, Maria looked out her window, gazing upon the world with new eyes. The streets below, a patchwork of lives in constant motion were no longer abstract patterns but a narrative in which she had etched her recent verse.

Maria realized the depth of the silence filling her home. The act of giving had cast a new light upon her solitude, a shadow now longed for the warmth of companionship. Her heart, fortified by the act of outreach, yearned now for a return—a voice, a touch, a presence.

Maria's campaign of goodwill, unbeknownst to her, began to weave a fabric of connection transcending the mere physicality of her envelopes and their contents. Stories emerged of individuals touched by her generosity—the surprised delight of old acquaintances, the bewildered smiles of former colleagues, the quiet contemplation of distant relatives—all united by the enigma of a five-dollar bill and a note speaking of a shared humanity.

Among the recipients was a young artist, Emilio, estranged from the well-heeled world of his upbringing, who saw in the note a sign to mend fences long thought beyond repair. Another, a philanthropist named Isabella, took inspiration to match Maria's gift a hundredfold, channeling her wealth into acts of generosity rippling outward with unabated enthusiasm.

In the following days, Maria's simple act became a seed sown in the fertile ground of society, taking root in ways she could not have imagined. The city, a mosaic of countless wills and destinies, pulsed with the undercurrent of her five-dollar bill's journey.

Stories returned to Maria carried on the winds of gossip and good news. In cafes and on street corners, people spoke of the mysterious notes and the resurgence of community spirit they inspired. "Who is behind this?" they asked. "What prompted such a gesture?" The city, it seemed, had found a new mystery to unravel, a new source of joy to ponder.

The answers to their questions lay in the silent chambers of Maria's heart. She, the orchestrator of this newfound happiness, remained within the walls of her estate, a queen in a self-imposed exile. Yet, she did not feel alone. Each story of a life touched by her act was a visitation, and each expression of gratitude was a companion at her table.

With brushstrokes inspired by Maria's note, Emilio, the artist, created a mural spanning the side of a building, a kaleidoscope of colors and faces telling the tale of interconnectedness. His reconciliation with his family, catalyzed by the five-dollar note, was depicted in the center—a visual homage to the cycle of giving and forgiveness.

Meanwhile, Isabella, the philanthropist, initiated a program in Maria's honor, though she knew her not. The Five for the Future fund became a beacon of support for the community, and each grant was a continuation of the goodwill Maria had begun. "Let us pay it forward" became the city's unofficial motto as more joined the movement to spread kindness.

In the quiet of her study, Maria watched the sunset. The joy she had brought to others returned to her in these twilight hours, a comforting embrace assuring her of her place in the world.

As night fell, Maria received a visitor. A young woman, moved by the stories of the five-dollar notes, had traced them back to their source. She stood at Maria's door, an emissary of all those Maria had reached. "You have given so much," the woman said, her eyes brimming with tears. "Now, let the city give back to you."

Invitations arrived for Maria, requests for her presence at gatherings and events, and letters of thanks from those she had touched. The city reached out its arms to her, drawing her back into the fold of life and society. Once a relic of the past, Maria became a celebrated figure, her wisdom and generosity the keys to a new kingdom of respect and admiration.

Amidst the accolades and attention, Maria found her greatest joy in the simple acts of kindness returned to her—a meal shared, a story exchanged, a moment of laughter in the company of newfound friends.

The echoes of Alhambra were no longer echoes—they were a vibrant symphony of lives touched, changed, and connected. The five-dollar bill, which had started in her hands, had traveled far and wide, weaving a story not of a solitary act but of a collective embrace, of the power of humanity to inspire and uplift through the simplest gestures.

Maria had begun with nothing more than a note and a five-dollar bill. Now, she was part of a kindness spanning the community, a testament to the enduring power of giving.

———

Chapter Eight
The Five-Dollar Change

Hyrum R. Patterson, owner and CEO of Foods for Life, Inc., stood by the floor-to-ceiling windows of his executive office, a panoramic view of the bustling city before him. His hands were clasped behind his back, fingers idly pressing the crisp texture of a five-dollar bill. The small note attached, penned by Maria Garcia, carried a heartfelt simplicity compared to the vastness of his corporate empire. For reasons eluding his usual analytical grasp, the gesture, diminutive as it was, intrigued him.

He let out a chuckle, the sound unfamiliar in the solitude of his office. With its unassuming script, the note had awakened a notion he'd not indulged in for years. Maria—a fleeting figure from social soirées, an old friend's wife—had challenged his well-honed perceptions of value and influence with a pen stroke and a meager five dollars.

He turned from the window, his eyes alighting upon the sophisticated trappings of his office—the art, the awards, the markers of success defining his world. Yet, in his hand, was an object, carrying a worth beyond its monetary face value. It symbolized a chain reaction of goodwill he, too, could propel forward.

As he contemplated the note's message, he realized the broader implications. It wasn't just about the money or even the act of giving. It was about leveraging influence for the greater good. With a swift movement, he pulled out his phone, initiating a call to his secretary.

"Alice, arrange a special board meeting for this Monday at noon. And let's make it interesting—a catered lunch, entertainment... I want to discuss a new initiative," he instructed, his voice imbued with an uncharacteristic buoyancy.

Monday arrived with a flourish of speculation. The executive boardroom, typically a theater of strategic battles and financial forecasts, had been transformed. The table was set with fine china, silver cutlery glinting in the light, and crystal glasses poised to be filled with champagne.

Hyrum watched as his board—men and women who navigated the currents of corporate America with him— filed in. Each was dressed to the nines, their expressions a blend of curiosity and amusement.

"Greetings," Hyrum began as the room became an expectant hush. "You might be wondering why I've called you here and why there's a five-dollar bill included in your invitations."

A wave of gentle laughter filled the room, and Hyrum allowed himself a small smile. He was not known for his levity; his reputation was built on shrewd business acumen and decisive leadership.

"All right," he continued, raising his hand to still the room. "I won't keep you in suspense. After lunch, I'll unveil a plan redefining the scope of our company's impact."

The lunch was exquisite, the chatter animated, and the quartet's music a lively backdrop to the convivial atmosphere. Yet, underlying it all was a current of anticipation—Hyrum was not known for idle gestures or wasted words.

Finally, as the last bites of dessert and the final sips of champagne were savored, Hyrum stood. He tapped his spoon against his glass, calling the room to order.

"Why the five-dollar bill?" he posed, his gaze sweeping across the faces of his trusted colleagues. "It's a symbol, a beginning. I've received such a bill, and it has inspired me to think about the influence we wield and how we might use it to better the world."

The room was rapt, and Hyrum felt the power of the moment. He outlined a vision—a program of philanthropy beginning with a simple five-dollar bill but would multiply and ripple outward, touching lives and enacting change.

"I propose we start an initiative," He declared, the five-dollar bill held up for all to see. "An initiative challenging each recipient to pay it forward, doubling, tripling its value for someone else."

A murmur of approval ran through the room. It was a bold idea, a venture into social responsibility writing a new chapter for Foods for Life, Inc., and for all those whom its unfolding legacy would touch.

The boardroom slowly emptied, leaving Hyrum in solitary contemplation of the ambitious undertaking lying ahead. In the quiet aftermath, the five-dollar bill, now symbolic of so much more than a simple monetary exchange, seemed to pulse with potential.

Hyrum spoke into the silence, an oath to himself and his pledge. The bill, once a simple token of kindness, had kindled a spark Hyrum was determined to fan into a flame—a flame casting light upon darkened doorsteps and bring warmth to those whose fortunes had turned cold.

No sooner had the idea begun to settle, like a fresh seed in fertile ground, than doubts crept in like unwelcome weeds. Could the initiative's enormity and reliance on human decency and altruism manifest the change he envisioned? Ever the strategist, He knew the peril of uncharted waters, yet the thrill of possibility outweighed the specter of risk.

In the following days, the plan, christened The Five Dollar Change, began to take shape. With his thoroughness, He crafted a blueprint for the initiative, engaging community leaders, philanthropists, and even skeptics in lively debate and discourse.

Alice Hickman, his trusted secretary, became a cornerstone of the endeavor; her efficiency and insight were invaluable as they outlined the logistics of spreading goodwill on such a vast scale. The twenty-two five-dollar bills, new and crisp, were to be the seeds from which this orchard of generosity would grow. They were dispatched across the nation, each bill accompanied by a letter from Hyrum, imploring its recipient to let it pass through their hands with an added measure of kindness.

The first reports of the five-dollar bills' journey began to trickle in. Stories of small acts of kindness, of bills turning into groceries for a struggling family, school supplies for underprivileged children, and even life-saving medication for those in need began to emerge. Each act was a link in a chain of compassion extending far beyond the gleaming skyscrapers and corporate boardrooms.

Winds of doubt and cynicism began to buffet the fledgling movement. Naysayers spoke of naivety, the impossibility of altering human nature, and the futility of throwing drops of goodwill into an ocean of need.

Hyrum doubled down on his commitment. He took to the airwaves, gave interviews, and wrote op-eds, his message clear and unwavering: change was a choice, a conscious act growing from the smallest of seeds.

He proclaimed on a national broadcast, the five-dollar bill held between his fingers. "We've ignited a movement gaining momentum with each passing day. And it's not because of me—it's because of us, all of us, choosing to believe in the power of kindness."

The Five Dollar Change was becoming a symphony of goodwill, its narrative winding through the lives it touched, a testament to the belief within each of us lies the power to enact profound change, five dollars at a time.

———

CHAPTER NINE
THE ROAD TO ELSEWHERE

Jack unfolded the five-dollar bill, running a thumb along its creases. He thought of Sandy and their daughter, Lilly—his heart constricted. The five-dollar bill was Sandy's last kindness, a reminder of what he once had and squandered.

He was hit with a wave of desperation. The irony wasn't lost on him—once a man of means, he was now a husk, contemplating the significance of a meager five dollars. Walking the streets aimlessly, Jack clutched the bill, Sandy's last gesture before she ushered him out of her life. Her face haunted him—the lines of stress he'd etched upon it, the eyes once sparkling with laughter now dulled with disappointment. He remembered Lilly, too—her cry, her laugh, how her tiny fingers had once curled around his own. They resonated within him, a cadence of what he'd lost. His thoughts were interrupted by the shattering realization he had nowhere to go. His family was lost to him, perhaps forever.

His walk took him to a shelter, a refuge for the downtrodden, and Jack shuffled toward it. He resisted the label he was about to assume—homeless. He wasn't like them, he argued inwardly; he wasn't one of the faceless many who'd fallen through society's cracks. But even as he argued, he knew he was lying to himself. He was one of them.

Inside the shelter, a different cold greeted him—one lacking the bite of the wind but chilled the spirit nonetheless. The coffee's aroma, however, promised a semblance of warmth. Jack made his way to the table and poured a cup, and the steam rising from the brew momentarily obscured his reflection in the window—a reflection he'd been avoiding.

As Jack cradled the warmth, a man approached him, hand outstretched—Mike Stockard. "I can tell by your shaking hand you could use some help," Mike said, and suddenly, Jack didn't feel so alone. In the community room, Jack listened to others share their battles with addiction, life, and their demons. A circle of men, strangers bound by their shared fall from grace, extended their hands.

He joined the circle, grasping hands roughened by hard luck and cold nights. He felt the pulse of collective strength flowing through them, a life force seeming alien to his current state. They shared stories, and he listened, the narratives mirroring his own.

When it was his turn to speak, words failed him. Instead, Jack pulled out the five-dollar bill, unfolding it with trembling hands for the group to see. "This... this was supposed to be my lifeline," he admitted, the whisper of his voice barely audible above the hum of the shelter.

The bill passed from hand to hand, each man looking at it not with greed but with understanding. They saw not money but a symbol—of failure, hope, and a chance to rise above. They encouraged Jack to use it, to make it the cornerstone of his new beginning.

Jack left the shelter with the five-dollar bill still in his pocket. At a crossroads, Jack stopped. He looked one way toward a liquor store, an all-too-familiar path, and the other led to the hospital: pain, both physical and emotional, nagged at him. A decision hung in the balance.

Jack chose the hospital, its sterile smell and white walls offering a clean slate. He approached the counter, "My shoulder hurts," he began, but the sight of others—some in more pain, some alone, some desperate—steered his course.

Jack didn't use the bill for his relief. Instead, he left it at the counter with a note. "Here's five dollars; give it to someone who could really use it. Make a difference," he said, with an uncharacteristic act of selflessness.

The bill, now in Anna's hands, the nurse whose shift had left her weary, saw not just currency but a message. The note with it—Jack's scrawled plea to make a difference—resonated with her. She pocketed the bill, the seed of a plan already taking root in her mind.

———

CHAPTER TEN
CATALYST FOR COMPASSION

Sheikh Mohammad Abu Baker al-Saud Wahhabi faced the most pleasant ritual of each day with gratitude to Allah, the Merciful, for all His generosity. He had enjoyed Ṣalāt al-Fajr—the first of the five daily Islamic prayers—and was ready for the thing pleasing him most about living in the desert—sunrise. His prayer occurred, as always, when he could first see a hair in the morning light; his knees warned him he was advancing in age. The desert sunrise filled him with joy for a new day, its beauty and eternal round convincing him of the greatness of his God, the only God, and of the power of the two families he represented—one on the military and administrative side (the monarchy), the al-Sauds, and the other on the religious and judicial side, the Wahhabi family.

The day's agenda also looked to be pleasant. His first visit in his desert tent was scheduled with the former American ambassador to the Kingdom, Maria Innocenta Garcia. Both of them were in their waning years, and he was feeling nostalgic. He and Maria had been best friends once upon a time, and he would have taken her as his second wife had she been agreeable. Long past her service to her great country, Maria still kept up cordial correspondence with the Sheikh.

The second item on his agenda was, for him, something of a trial of his efforts to be accepting of other persons not like him and not generally seen socially by members of the Saudi family with its more than 5,000 princes. It was a Jew, Abraham ben Cohen, holder of the priesthood of Aaron, which both religions held sacred. Abraham was a scholar of both faiths and the history of the lands they occupied. He enjoyed his conversations with the rabbi and looked forward to the verbal jousting in which they sought one-upmanship on their religious and historical interests.

A minor difference in his agenda's routine took place. Both old friends arrived at the same time by prearrangement.

"As-salaam 'alaykum," he said to the pair of elderly friends and treated them to a smile borne of fondness.

"Wa 'alaykum as-salaam," they replied in unison, and the three shook hands in the Western fashion.

The three old friends shared a small glass of pomegranate juice, fresh baklava, and Katayef, a sweet and savory treat made of fried batter filled with cream, cheese, and nuts and topped with syrup. Al Wahhabi was famous for his sweet tooth, so the servants deep-fried the treat before drenching it in syrup for extra sweetness.

The friends sighed in simultaneous satisfaction and satiety and got down to business.

"I know both of you have come a long way for this happy meeting, and none of us is getting any younger. Tell me, pray, in the name of the Omnipotent, what brings you all this way?"

Rabbi Cohen nodded in deference to the august dowager from the United States, and she took the lead.

"My dear old friend, by the sheerest and best of coincidences, Abraham and I received a most interesting gift recently—the same thing, both coming from anonymous sources. Let me show the messages we received and a photocopy of the gifts themselves."

She handed him the two envelopes, and he opened them. They contained identical messages and photocopies of five-dollar bills of US currency. He was astute enough to notice the serial numbers differed, but he was confused. He asked, "I trust you know I am one of the wealthiest men in the world, my dear friends, and I do not say it to boast. But why have you presented me with photocopies of such small sums? Not that I am greedy or expect more."

Maria and Abraham chuckled.

She responded to Sheikh Mohammad, "And also among the most humble."

She smiled as she said it, and the three friends shared a comradely laugh.

"Read the rest of the note."

He put on his dime-store readers and said aloud, "And pass it on."

Letting it sink in for a moment, she said, "Are we all on the same page?"

"We are. What's the plan, my friends?"

"We both have large mailing lists, email lists, texting friends, Facebook friends, and a presence on TikTok, X, and Instagram. We presume you do as well."

"I admit to having become trendy. In addition, I am amply represented on LinkedIn, YouTube, Snapchat, and Skype, all popular in the Middle East. Together, we just about cover the population of the earth."

"Let's get to work," Maria and Abraham said in unison, and they set about with zeal.

As the morning progressed and the tent began to warm under the desert sun, the trio delved deeper into the mechanics of their initiative. The Sheikh leaned forward, his hands clasped in determination. "Let's not just spark a ripple of kindness; let's create a wave," he declared, his voice resonant with passion and purpose.

Always practical and focused, Maria began outlining the logistical framework necessary to realize their vision. "We'll need a robust system to manage this campaign. Tracking, coordination, and communication will be key. Each bill and each letter must be carefully logged to ensure we can follow its journey and impact."

She suggested setting up a central command within the Sheikh's estate, utilizing his extensive resources. This would include a dedicated team for logistics, a communications group to handle outreach and media interactions, and a technical team to develop and manage the digital platform where the stories of generosity would be shared globally.

Abraham, whose thoughts often turned toward the ethical implications of their actions, raised a point about the personal touch in their approach. "It's important each recipient feels personally selected and valued," he noted. "These aren't just random acts of charity; they are part of a greater narrative we are weaving. The letters should reflect a narrative, embodying our hopes and intentions clearly and inspiringly."

The Sheikh nodded in agreement and suggested personalizing each letter with a message explaining the initiative and sharing their motivation for starting this movement. "We should each sign the initial batch of letters," he proposed. "It will lend a personal touch and a sense of unity to our cause."

With a plan taking shape, they turned their attention to the list of potential recipients. This list had been carefully curated to include influential figures across various sectors: philanthropy, entertainment, business, and grassroots organizations. Each person was chosen for their potential to act as a catalyst within their community and sphere of influence.

Maria took the lead in discussing the distribution strategy. "We'll start with a pilot phase," she suggested. "Selecting a diverse group from different continents will allow us to test our approach and make adjustments before we expand further."

She outlined the distribution plan, which involved sending packages via courier to ensure each bill and letter was delivered securely. "We'll use tracking numbers for each package, allowing us to monitor their delivery and receipt. This data will be crucial for our follow-up phase and for adjusting our strategies in real-time."

The technical aspect of the initiative was particularly crucial. They contracted a leading software development company to build the digital platform. This platform would serve multiple functions: it would allow recipients to upload their stories, photos, or videos; provide a public-facing website where these stories could be shared; and include a private backend for the team to monitor progress and engage with participants.

Abraham was tasked with the design of the platform's content. "The site should be more than just functional; it should inspire those who visit it," he said. "It should visually convey the journey of the bills and the stories they've catalyzed, providing a tangible sense of the global community we're building."

As they discussed the website's features, Maria emphasized the importance of accessibility. "The platform must be user-friendly, available in multiple languages, and accessible on various devices. We want no barriers to participation or sharing the stories we collect."

The conversation then shifted to potential challenges they might face. The Sheikh pointed out the logistical complexities of working across different legal and cultural environments. "We must ensure our initiative respects local laws and customs," he stated. "This will require careful research and possibly local partners who can guide us."

Maria agreed, noting the importance of privacy and data protection. "We need to safeguard the personal information of all participants. Trust will be a cornerstone of this campaign's success."

By mid-afternoon, the tent was filled with the vibrant energy of collaboration and creativity. The Sheikh, Maria, and Abraham reviewed their comprehensive plan, each component now clearly outlined and assigned. They agreed to meet regularly to oversee the initiative's progress and to adapt the strategy as needed based on real-world feedback and the evolving landscape of their project.

As they concluded the meeting, they each felt a profound sense of commitment to their cause. This wasn't just about distributing money or collecting stories; it was about igniting a global movement of kindness and human connection.

As the desert sky transitioned from the soft hues of twilight into the deep blues of evening, Sheikh Mohammad, Maria, and Abraham remained seated outside the tent, each contemplating the significant journey they had embarked upon. The Sheikh broke the silence, his voice reflecting a mix of determination and optimism. "We have planted the seeds of something truly monumental today," he said, looking out across the dunes bathed in moonlight.

Maria nodded, her thoughts already approaching the logistical challenges they would face. "The road ahead will require careful navigation," she acknowledged. "We must remain vigilant, adaptive, and above all, committed to our principles." She understood while their initiative was rooted in simplicity—a five-dollar bill and a message—their ambition to spark a global wave of kindness was a complex endeavor testing their resolve and resources.

Abraham, ever the reflective soul, considered the deeper implications of their work. "We are calling upon people to connect, share, and extend kindness beyond the comfortable boundaries of their lives," he mused. "In doing so, we are spreading generosity and fostering a greater sense of global community." His thoughts were on the transformative power of collective action, a theme he often explored in his writings and lectures.

The trio discussed the importance of maintaining a narrative resonating with diverse audiences. They agreed on the necessity of regular storytelling updates on social media, highlighting inspiring actions and the chain reactions of kindness. The Sheikh suggested launching a monthly feature story, focusing on particularly impactful stories illustrating their initiative's broad reach and deep impact.

As the evening wore on, they focused on the potential cultural and logistical hurdles they might encounter. "We need to be culturally sensitive and inclusive in our approach," Maria emphasized, drawing from her extensive experience in international relations. "Each region, each community has its nuances. Our success will depend on how well we understand and respect these differences."

The night deepened around them, the stars overhead shining brightly against the dark sky. The desert, a vast expanse of solitude and tranquility, seemed the perfect backdrop for their reflections on human kindness and connectivity. As they each retired to their quarters, thoughts of the future filled their minds—visions of kindness crossing borders, languages, and cultures to weave a mosaic of global unity.

The conclusion of their meeting under the desert stars had been just the beginning. What followed was a journey none of them could have imagined—one proving the power of a small gesture to ignite a global change, demonstrating even the simplest act of passing on a five-dollar bill could unite the world in a shared narrative of hope and humanity.

———

CHAPTER ELEVEN
JACK'S CANVAS

Jack's eyes fluttered open, the haunting echo of the shelter's late-night murmurs still bouncing off the walls in his mind. He lay there on the cot that had become his confessor, his cradle between past transgressions and the hope for redemption. He moved slowly, muscles tensing against the chill of withdrawal, his every breath an effort to stave off the physical protest of a body too long marinated in alcohol. Yet, in this shrine to second chances, it was here where Jack's rebirth had begun, where the remembrance of Sandy's last act—an exchange of a mere five-dollar bill—had kindled a flame determined to outlast the darkness of his past.

Mike, a kindred spirit whose scars spoke a language of struggle and survival, stood by Jack's side. Mike was a pillar, a sentinel who taught Jack not just to survive but to live with courage only by witnessing the abyss and stepping back into the light.

A contrast caught his eye as Jack moved to fold the laundered blankets. A colorful flyer on the community board screamed for attention. It was an advertisement for a local art competition seeking entries depicting the theme of The Power of Giving. The prize was not monumental, but it felt like a call to Jack. Here was a chance to express the inexpressible—to show the world what Sandy's last gift meant to him.

Within these walls, another soul found solace, a newcomer whose story wove into the fabric of the shelter's history. Dinah May stepped into the fold, her spirit bruised by life's unkind rhythms. The shelter's regime was a challenge, a stark contrast to the chaos she had known. Yet, she watched Jack, the man with eyes like storm clouds parting, and found an unexpected anchor in his steadfastness.

In a twist of fate, Thomas, the pastor whose church had become a haven for Jack, discovered an affinity with Dinah May. Her story, marked by stumbles and triumphs, echoed in the hymns and sermons of his church. Thomas' invitation to her was simple: "Come and see. There's a family here not of blood but of spirit."

Dinah May took a hesitant step into the warmth of the congregation. There, amidst the melodies of faith and fellowship, she found a canvas large enough to paint her gratitude—the church's community outreach program.

As Jack prepared his entry for the art competition, using every ounce of his newfound purpose, he realized the piece was not just his own. It was a mosaic of many—the warmth in Mike's eyes, the quiet strength in Dinah May's resolve, the open arms of Thomas' congregation.

The shelter's common room, which served as Jack's makeshift studio, was a patchwork of lives in transition; each individual had a canvas of frayed edges and half-finished stories. Amidst this, Jack seemed an anomaly with his paints and brushes. His hands, which once fumbled with the simplicity of day-to-day sobriety, now moved with unexpected grace across his canvas. Those in the shelter had grown used to the sight, but it was a quiet marvel to an outsider.

Dinah May stood beside him, watching as the painting began to take form. "I didn't know you were an artist, Jack," she remarked, a note of surprise in her voice.

Jack's chuckle was soft, humbled. "I wasn't. Not really. But I guess when you hit rock bottom, you find parts of yourself buried deep." He dipped his brush into a swirl of paint. "Found these old art supplies in the storage. Figured I'd put them to use."

"So, you taught yourself?" Dinah May's question was tinged with a blend of admiration and curiosity.

Jack nodded. "Well, Mike there," he gestured with his chin toward a middle-aged man watching from the doorway, "found me a few books on painting. And Thomas, the pastor, hooked me up with some online tutorials. I used to paint, but my life took another turn. But will all this, it's coming back."

Dinah May's eyes widened as she understood. "You've created something from almost nothing."

"That's just it," Jack said, gesturing at the canvas, "it's like us here. From nothing, or what seems like it, we find light, color, hope."

The others gathered around, drawn in by the conversation about creation from desolation. Each person added their piece, their interpretation of the emerging image. It was becoming a communal piece of art.

As Jack added a stroke, Irene, who seldom spoke up, pointed at a particular blend of hues. "That corner there, it's just like dawn. Like the start of something new."

Jack's eyes met hers in the dimly lit room. "It is. Each day here is like a new dawn. We mess up, we start over."

The conversation ebbed and flowed around Jack's art. Each person saw something different in it—some a beginning, others an end, some of struggles and victories.

In the corner stood a new arrival. "What good is a painting in a place like this?" he asked, his voice rough-edged, untrusting.

Jack set down his brush. "A painting in a place like this is a reminder. We're more than our circumstances. This—" he gestured to the painting, "—is proof we're still here, still fighting, still dreaming."

The skeptic walked closer, peering at the canvas. Slowly, his expression softened. "Maybe," he conceded, "there's something to it."

The very act of entering the competition was a win for Jack, a personal victory over doubts and fears shackling him to a past he was learning to see through a different light. With the encouragement of the shelter community—Mike's steady support, Dinah May's quiet admiration, and the skeptical newcomer's reluctant belief—Jack submitted his piece.

The day of the results was filled with an undercurrent of anticipation in the shelter. No matter the outcome, Jack's painting had already achieved something remarkable—it had united the group, giving them a shared focus, a collective whisper of "what if?"

When the winners were announced, the shelter was abuzz with nervous energy. Jack's name was called—not for the grand prize, but for a special mention, an acknowledgment of the raw, emotive power his piece conveyed. It wasn't just an accolade for his newfound skill but for the story the painting told, a testament to the journey from shadow into light each person at the shelter was intimately familiar with.

The competition organizers visited the shelter surprising them all. Moved by Jack's story and the painting's narrative, they decided to feature his work in an upcoming exhibition dedicated to showcasing the therapeutic power of art in recovery and rehabilitation.

Jack stood before his friends and family in spirit, if not by blood, as they congratulated him. There were handshakes, pats on the back, and, for some, a few tears refusing to be held back. The recognition was sweet, yes, but the journey—the journey was sweeter. It wasn't about the accolade; it was about the process, the courage to enter, and the joy of sharing his vision with others.

———

CHAPTER TWELVE
A PALETTE OF NEW HORIZONS

Sandy's apartment whispered of a night steeped in transformation. As the first shy rays of dawn tiptoed through the blinds, Sandy awoke, a silent observer of the day's soft commencement. The apartment, once a stage for the evening's tense drama, now stood serene, a tableau pregnant with the unspoken promise of new beginnings. Today marked not just another turn of the earth but the first page of a new chapter in the book of her life.

She rose, her movements deliberate, to brew a fresh pot of coffee. The simple ritual, once a shared comfort, was now a solitary act of independence. The scent wafted through the rooms, a signal the night had retreated, and life awaited their command. In the stillness, Sandy found clarity and, with it, a resolve not just to exist but to reclaim her life, one unburdened by past shadows.

Lilly, her daughter, remained nestled in the curve of the couch, clutching her bear—a sentinel of soft fur guarding her dreams. Sandy's heart swelled at the sight, her child's innocence a stark contrast to the complexities of the world she had to navigate. The young mother pondered how to sculpt this new existence for Lilly, to tell her stories of heroines and high adventures, not of nights filled with discord and decisions too heavy for her tender years.

Sandy set out to ensure her determination was not a fleeting whisper, but a declaration etched into the fabric of reality. In the local library, a sanctuary of silence and knowledge, Sandy sought resources to aid her journey forward. Among the shelves, she met Ayesha, the librarian.

Ayesha noticed Sandy's intent in her search and approached. "Is everything okay?" she asked, her voice a blend of welcome and curiosity.

"I'm looking for job listings, perhaps some guides on resume building," Sandy replied, her hands brushing the spines of books.

Ayesha's face brightened with understanding. "You're in luck. We're hosting a job seekers' workshop this afternoon. Why don't you join us?"

The offer was a balm to Sandy's uncertainty. She nodded, gratitude painting her features. "Thank you, I will."

Lilly ambled up as they chatted. Ayesha greeted her with a smile, producing a coloring book from behind the desk. "For our youngest guest," she said, winking.

Greta Olsen's hurried entrance momentarily disrupted the quiet of the library. Sandy's neighbor's face was flushed from the haste, and her hands clutched a flyer.

"Sandy, dear," she panted, catching her breath. "I saw this and thought of you immediately because of your interest in gardening."

The flyer advertised a community garden seeking volunteers. "They offer training and sometimes jobs to those who help out. It's an opportunity, especially for Lilly, to play and learn," Greta explained, her eyes gleaming excitedly at the prospect.

Sandy's heart skipped with the possibility. "Greta, this is wonderful, thank you."

Sandy and Greta, with Lilly in tow, ventured to the community garden, where the air buzzed with the hum of conversation and the earthy scent of soil and growth. They were greeted by Marco, a man whose hands were as rugged as the garden beds he tended but whose smile softened his appearance.

"We believe in nurturing growth in plants and people," Marco said, his voice rich with the melody of his Italian heritage. "You willing to learn?"

Sandy glanced at Lilly, whose excitement was barely contained. "We are," she said, her words not just an acceptance but a commitment.

As they settled into the garden rhythm, hands dirtied by soil, Lilly's laughter mingled with the birdsong. Sandy's dedication and hard work quickly caught the attention of Marco and the other volunteers. She felt a sense of belonging and purpose in the garden, a stark contrast to the turmoil she had left behind.

One afternoon, after weeks of volunteering, Sandy pulled off her gardening gloves, the dirt ingrained in the fabric a testament to her day's work. She wiped her hand on her jeans and reached out to Ms. Hampton, a philanthropist who had been observing the garden's progress.

"Thank you," Sandy said, her smile blossoming like the roses around them. "I love working in the garden and would be so grateful for the chance to share it with children. My own daughter, Lilly, calls the gardens her Fairy Land."

Ms. Hampton's expression softened, her gaze wandering toward the vibrant blooms. "I rather like the idea," she admitted. "You come highly recommended by Marco for the job. I wonder if I might meet your Lilly and have her tell me about her 'Fairy Land.' I have a young daughter too and would love to have her included in our little venture."

As they strolled through the maze of marigolds and ferns, Sandy's thoughts drifted to Lilly, whose imagination turned every shadow into a fairy and every leaf into a whispering sprite. The gardens were not just plots of land but gateways to worlds unseen.

The park was a sanctuary for Sandy, more so after the tumult of her separation from Jack. She first noticed the poster pinned haphazardly to the corkboard near the entrance. The painting depicted a couple under the wisteria archway, uncannily resembling her and Jack. The poster announced an upcoming charity event in the park. While reading it, Sandy remembered the day after she had ended things with Jack, when she applied for her current job. The role hadn't turned out as expected, but it had brought her here.

When the organizers visited the park, Sandy learned the event would feature artworks to be auctioned for charity, including a piece by a homeless man—Jack. The revelation rocked her, threading fear and curiosity through her heart.

Despite her apprehensions, her curiosity about Jack's transformation into an artist and the details of the Five-dollar Fund compelled her to stay for the event. She resolved to remain behind the scenes, avoiding Jack at all costs.

The event day arrived, and the park transformed into a gallery under the open sky. Sandy busied herself with last-minute preparations, her heart thrumming with a mix of dread and excitement. Her plan to remain unseen was challenged when she overheard visitors praising the heartfelt artwork by the once-forgotten artist.

Sandy's mind was a whirlpool of emotions in the heart of the bustling event. The park, usually a place of solace and rejuvenation, was now transformed into a vibrant hub of activity. Art enthusiasts, curious locals, and philanthropists mingled, their voices blending into a lively hum.

As she skirted the edges of the gathering, her gaze fell upon a painting. It was a depiction of the park's old maple tree, under which she had shared many moments with Jack. The strokes were rough, charged with emotion, and achingly familiar. Sandy felt her breath catch. "Could this be Jack's work too?"

Nearby, Ms. Hampton, who had been observing Sandy's distraction, approached with a gentle touch on the shoulder. "It's captivating, isn't it?" she said, her eyes reflecting a spark of curiosity. "The artist must have a deep connection with this place, just as you do."

As they conversed, a young girl tugged at Ms. Hampton's dress. "Mommy, look! That lady looks just like the princess in the painting!" she exclaimed, pointing excitedly at Sandy.

"Yes, darling, perhaps she does." Turning to Sandy, she whispered, "My daughter, Emma, has quite the imagination. Just like Lilly, I suppose."

Their conversation was interrupted by the announcement the next set of artworks was about to be auctioned.

Ms. Hampton excused herself, taking Emma to view the paintings, leaving Sandy to her thoughts.

Sandy decided to confront her past. She moved through the crowd until she stood before the next painting. It was another of Jack's depicting two figures walking away from each other, their shadows merging with the twilight.

Standing behind a group of onlookers, Jack watched Sandy's reaction to his work. His journey from the depths of despair had been littered with challenges and triumphs. Seeing Sandy here, engaged with his art, sparked a mixture of pride and regret.

As she stood before one particularly poignant piece, Jack appeared beside her. Their silent, heartfelt encounter spoke volumes. Old wounds resurfaced, and unspoken grievances threatened to overshadow the moment. "Can we ever truly move past our history?" Sandy wondered.

Jack broke the silence. "I'm glad you came, Sandy. This work... it's my way of making amends."

Sandy looked into his eyes, searching for sincerity. "I see that, Jack. But it's not just about the past. It's about moving forward."

They talked, revisiting painful memories and sharing their hopes for the future.

CHAPTER THIRTEEN
THE COMPASS OF KINDNESS

Anna sat in the hospital cafeteria, her fingers drumming on the table. Beside her half-eaten club sandwich lay the five-dollar bill, folded neatly, a silent testament to a promise yet to be fulfilled. She sipped her herbal tea, its steam curling into the air like a beacon summoning her resolve. This bill, this small piece of paper charged with so much hope, had to be passed along with intent. It had to spark a movement, no matter how small, growing into something meaningful.

George Hedges, known for his brisk walk and even brisker decisions, approached the counter, his gaze fixed on the agenda clutched in his hand. Spotting Anna, his brow lifted in surprise, a silent question hanging between them.

"Hey, George!" Anna called, her voice slicing through the cafeteria's hum. "I've got a project I need your help with."

George set aside his plans, his curiosity piqued as he slid into the seat opposite her. "What's up?" he inquired, leaning forward.

Anna pushed the five-dollar bill toward him, the note from Jack resting atop it. "This isn't just money," she began, her eyes alight with the ember of an idea. "I want to start something. Five Dollar Day. A day where we put kindness into action and do something, however small, with five dollars to help someone else. It could be anything—paying for a meal, buying a blanket, or even offering a listening ear. We document these acts, share them, and watch the ripple effect grow."

George regarded the bill, the gears turning behind his eyes. "Five Dollar Day, huh? Grassroots generosity, Anna. It could be powerful."

With George on board, Anna's idea began to take shape. George, well-versed in the language of grants and the music of community relations, saw the kindness in Anna's proposal and the potential for a broader impact. "Let's pitch it to the hospital board," he suggested, the administrative wheels already turning in his head. "We'll need a plan, something they can see, touch, believe in."

Anna's smile broadened. "I was hoping you'd say that."

As Anna and George plotted the birth of Five Dollar Day, the hospital corridors thrummed with the lives of those on the edges of society's concern. A young man with a worn backpack sat in a quiet corner of the emergency room, his face a canvas of worry lines. Noah had come in with a persistent cough keeping him from his job at the shelter—the same shelter Jack had stumbled into. Noah's story was one of quiet strength, a life pieced together after a childhood spent in foster care, a testament to the resolve of the human spirit.

After being seen by the doctor, Noah was given a prescription he couldn't afford. He slumped into the plastic chair, feeling the world's weight pressing upon his chest. It was then Anna noticed Noah's defeated posture during her break, with the Five Dollar Day plan fresh in her mind.

Approaching him with the gentleness she reserved for the most fragile patients, she asked, "Is everything okay?"

Noah looked up, his eyes betraying his pride. "It's just a prescription," he admitted. "I can't... I don't have the money for it."

Anna's heart twisted. Here was the very essence of her project, sitting before her, wrestling with pride and need. Reaching into her pocket, she felt the texture of the five-dollar bill. It wasn't enough to cover the cost but could be a start.

Anna was about to offer Noah the bill when George approached, a wide grin splitting his face. "The board loved it, Anna! Five Dollar Day is a go. And guess what? They want to kickstart it by covering prescriptions for those in need this month."

Noah's eyes widened in disbelief. "Really?"

"Yes," Anna beamed, "and it all started with this five-dollar bill." She handed him the bill, not as payment but as a symbol of what was possible. "This is for you to pay forward when you can, in your own way."

Noah clutched the bill, the reality of the moment sinking in. "I... I don't know what to say."

"Just say you'll be part of Five Dollar Day when you're ready," Anna said, her heart swelling with the knowledge this was only the beginning.

With Five Dollar Day now officially endorsed, Anna's shift ended on a high note, reverberating through her steps as she left the hospital. She glanced at Noah, now speaking with a social worker, the five-dollar bill a secret promise in his pocket. Her project had found its legs quicker than she dared hope, and now it sprinted toward the future she was eager to shape.

In a nearby neighborhood, the impact of the five-dollar bill began to unfold in a manner nobody at the hospital could have anticipated. Jasmine, who ran the local bookstore, had noticed the increased foot traffic. People weren't just browsing but looking for books on kindness, social movements, and changing the world one step at a time.

Jasmine suggested several titles: *The Kindness Curriculum: Stop Bullying Before It Starts* by Judith Anne Rice, *A Little SPOT of Kindness!* by Diane Alber, *Tomorrow I'll Be Kind* by Jessica Hische, *Superbuns* by Diane Kredensor, *It's Brave to Be Kind* by Natasha, *Listening With My Heart: A Story of Kindness and Self-Compassion* by Gabi Garcia, and *Be Kind* by Pat Zietlow Miller. She placed them in the storefront and watched customers leave with books cradled like newfound treasures.

Among the visitors was a young teacher, Elena, who taught at the elementary school down the street. She picked up a copy of Be Kind, and an idea took root. Her third graders, she thought, could use a lesson in kindness—a perfect match for Five Dollar Day.

Elena approached Jasmine. "I want to start a classroom project for Five Dollar Day," she explained. "Could you help me find more books like this?"

Jasmine's lips curved into a smile. "I think we can do better. Let's start a book club—Pages of Kindness. We can get the kids reading and doing."

While Jasmine and Elena were plotting to sow seeds of goodwill in young minds, the city council was amid heated discussions. Budget cuts loomed, threatening the fabric of community services, including the local shelter where Noah worked and where Jack had found temporary solace.

Councilman Richard Hart, whose stern face often hid his soft heart, listened as the numbers were presented. The shelter's funds were on the chopping block, the figures stark on the bright screen. But Richard had seen Five Dollar Day's inception, had witnessed the hospital's embrace of this grassroots initiative, and something within him stirred.

Richard took the floor at the next council meeting, his voice resounding through the chamber. "What is the cost of kindness?" he asked his peers. "We can lead by example, invest in projects like Five Dollar Day, and ensure our shelters remain a beacon of hope."

A murmur ran through the room, a mix of skepticism and intrigue. Richard, however, was not deterred. He spoke of Anna's project, the man who inspired it, the teacher eager to educate through it, and the countless lives being touched, potentially altered, by a mere five dollars.

As Richard spoke, a live stream of the council meeting played on the TV in a small diner downtown. The patrons, sipping coffee and digging into late breakfasts, listened. Among them was Lydia, a retired nurse whose heart had never left the halls of the hospital where she had served for thirty years. She watched as Richard championed the cause close to her heart.

Lydia knew the power of community. She knew, too, the faces of those who frequented the shelter; they were not just the homeless or the lost; they were friends, and they were familiar. By the time Richard's speech concluded, Lydia was determined to act. She left the diner with purpose, her mission clear.

Arriving at the shelter, Lydia found Noah back from the hospital, his expression one of worry about the fate of his place of work. Lydia approached, her gait steady, her resolve firmer.

"Noah," she called out, and he turned. "I just heard the city council. We need to mobilize for Five Dollar Day. We need to show them what this shelter means to the community."

"Let's do it."

The challenge was set, and the city rose to meet it. Five Dollar Day became more than a moment; it became a movement, a testament to the power of empathy and action, to the belief change doesn't always start with grand gestures but with small, deliberate acts of kindness.

As autumn came with the rustle of changing leaves, the city witnessed the harvest of kindness seeded by the Five Dollar Day movement. Once splintered by unseen battles and silent struggles, the community thrummed with a new pulse. Mrs. Henderson's challenge had not just been met; it had been embraced and multiplied, each act of kindness fueling another, each donation sparking further generosity.

The shelter stood in the heart of this reborn community, no longer on the brink of closure but thriving as a center of hope and transformation. Kathryn's art classes had become a cornerstone of expression for many who sought solace and a voice through color and form. The walls, adorned with stories painted from the soul, spoke to all who entered—whispering of resilience, echoing strength, and shouting joy.

The pages of kindness turned in classrooms and homes alike as books on empathy and social change flew off the shelves of Jasmine's bookstore. Elena's students, armed with knowledge and fueled by compassion, embarked on projects reaching far beyond the confines of their classroom, touching lives and teaching lessons grades could never measure.

Alex, the journalist, found his career defined by the stories of Five Dollar Day. His articles, once a simple job, had become a mission—a chronicle of humanity's capacity for goodness, a narrative mirroring the very essence of the movement itself.

And at the heart of it all was Anna, whose simple gesture with a five-dollar bill had sparked this mosaic of interwoven lives and stories. As she walked through the city, witnessing the kindness she had kindled, a profound sense of connection enveloped her. She realized the five-dollar bill, now worn and passed through countless hands, was more than currency—it was a vessel of communal spirit, an emblem of the change one small act of kindness could make in a vast world.

This was the power of kindness—it knew no boundaries, no end. It traveled, transformed, and transcended, becoming more than anyone could have imagined, leaving an indelible mark on society and the heart of a city reborn.

———

CHAPTER FOURTEEN
THE SEEDS OF GENEROSITY

Manny remembered the three crisp five-dollar bills he had received back at a small store because the cashier didn't have a ten. He had spent one on gas at the Quick Stop and kept the other two in his wallet. The idea of passing forward this seemingly minor amount had been inspired by a conversation overheard at the homeless shelter where he volunteered. A story of a five-dollar bill serving as a lifeline had resonated with him. It wasn't just currency but a beacon of hope, a testament to human kindness.

Manny decided the remaining bills in his wallet were not meant to stay there. He planned to give them away. Manny, short for Emmanuel, which meant 'God with us,' found it fitting he should be the bearer of good news or at least a good note. His mind replayed the brief moments spent at the doorstep of Maria's sprawling, vine-covered mansion. He had slid the envelope with the five-dollar bill under her door with the note, "Dear Maria," it read, "This is a gift that keeps on giving. Enjoy your day and your life. Pass it on and make someone else happy."

Manny knew Maria only from a distance. She was an older woman who lived down the street from him. Her house was a familiar sight in the neighborhood. He occasionally saw her coming and going. They had never formally met, but Manny had heard about her through conversations with neighbors. They spoke of Maria's long history in the community, her kindness, and the quiet strength she possessed.

Curiosity and a sense of admiration had led Manny to choose Maria as one of the recipients of his five-dollar bill. He imagined her surprise and the slow smile spreading across her face as she read his words. The other letter had gone to a gentleman who lived a few blocks away, someone Manny knew only from the books he ordered about history and faith.

As Manny reflected on these moments, he felt a deep sense of fulfillment. Each act of kindness was a tribute to the principles he held dear. The thought of Maria receiving his note and continuing the cycle of generosity filled him with hope for a world where small acts of kindness could spark significant change.

————

Chapter Fifteen
Convergence of Intentions

Having performed his morning prayers, Sheikh Mohammad Abu Baker al-Saud Wahhabi felt a sense of tranquility. He had always found solace in these quiet moments, the world still and expectant. This morning, however, carried an undercurrent of anticipation.

The desert meeting with his friends, Maria Innocenta Garcia and Abraham ben Cohen, had been more than a reunion. The five-dollar bills they each received had sparked a movement gaining momentum beyond their expectations. Little did they know, their acts of kindness were weaving a global collage of goodwill, a narrative transcending borders and beliefs.

In a sleek, modern office far removed from the desert's simplicity, Sacha Claes, dressed in his customary grey suit, couldn't contain his excitement. "Ya Salam!" he exclaimed. "Now, who would have thought they, themselves, would do our work and pave the way for us so clearly? Just when we thought we'd have to postpone our target, they came and accelerated the whole process for us. If they only knew." He laughed, the irony of the situation too delicious to ignore.

The five-dollar good deeds were placing the power in their hands, unwittingly facilitating their grand plan.

Rayan Ysebaert, the mastermind behind this scheme, remained composed, his dark eyes gleaming with calculated satisfaction. "Right, Sacha. We got them, and they don't know it yet. We should thank them for herding the flocks together so we can fence them in, together with their flocks." He clasped his hands together, his voice steady and unyielding. "Instead of putting our next project on hold, we can proceed at full speed. Get your generals together, and let's start the fencing-in process."

Sacha, Yanis Elsen, Jules Fontaine, and Martine Janssens departed the office, ready to summon their generals and execute the next phase of their plan. Yanis, avoiding his office phone for secrecy, called Monique Kusters from his cell, arranging a meeting at the Hilton Towers. The gravity of the task at hand required absolute discretion.

Monique arrived punctually, her demeanor reflecting the seriousness of the mission. Yanis laid out the plan, which she would refine and execute with precision. Their goal: to manipulate the goodwill generated by the five-dollar bills, convincing the participants to unite under a new government and prescribed religion.

Unbeknownst to Rayan and his cohort, the five-dollar project IT team got word of the plot and mobilized their resources to resist this sinister plan. Software experts were enlisted, and warnings were sent to Cohen and Garcia, urging them to inform the Sheikh. They swiftly changed website access, advising participants to reject any offers or threats from third-party entities. A declaration was posted, clearly stating the original purpose and plan, urging vigilance and resistance against manipulation.

Back in the desert, Sheikh Wahhabi, Garcia, and Cohen discussed the unexpected revelations. "We must protect this movement," Cohen said, his voice firm with conviction. "It was meant to spread kindness, not control."

Garcia nodded in agreement. "We need to ensure our message remains pure and untainted. Let's inform all participants and safeguard our initiative."

The three friends, united by a common cause, vowed to thwart any attempts to hijack their movement. Their resolve was unyielding, their spirits fortified by the shared belief in the power of kindness.

In a high-rise building, the schemers were in full swing, unaware of the counteractions set in motion. In Suite 704 of the Hilton Towers, Monique Kusters meticulously reviewed the plan laid out by Yanis. Her fingers tapped rhythmically on the laptop keyboard, updating protocols and directives. "This software is powerful," she muttered, "we just need to leverage it correctly to influence the masses."

Meanwhile, in a small, cluttered apartment on the other side of town, the five-dollar project IT team of tech-savvy friends was deep in discussion. Paula, an expert coder, had found a vulnerability in Rayan's software. "We can exploit this to block their communications," she said, her voice tinged with urgency. "If we act fast, we can prevent them from manipulating the participants."

Richard Hart, a seasoned activist, leaned forward. "We need to be careful. One misstep, and they'll know we're onto them. We should also prepare a counter-narrative, something reinforcing the original message of kindness and generosity."

As the counter-effort gathered momentum, Sacha Claes grew suspicious. He noticed anomalies in their software's performance—glitches seeming too deliberate to be mere coincidences. "Yanis, something's not right. Our systems are being tampered with."

Yanis frowned, "Get Martine and Jules on this. We can't afford any disruptions now." He dialed Monique's number, urgency in his tone, "We need to tighten security. Increase surveillance on all key participants. I want eyes and ears everywhere."

Back in the desert, the trio of friends—Sheikh Wahhabi, Garcia, and Cohen—had mobilized their networks. They sent out messages to all known participants, warning them of the impending threats and urging them to remain steadfast.

Evelyn, the Quick Stop clerk who had passed on the original five dollars, received one of these messages. She read it with growing alarm. The small act of kindness she had facilitated had grown into something much larger than she ever imagined, now under threat from unseen forces. Determined to help, she reached out to her customers, explaining the situation and rallying support.

In a café in downtown New York, Evelyn met with a group of concerned citizens. Among them was Liam, a journalist known for his investigative prowess. "We need to get the word out," Evelyn urged. "People need to know about this conspiracy."

Liam nodded, "I can write an exposé. But we'll need concrete evidence. Can you connect me with someone on the inside?"

Evelyn thought for a moment. "There's a tech group working to counteract this. I'll try to get you in touch with them."

Across town, Monique was on edge. The software glitches persisted, and surveillance footage revealed suspicious activities. "They're onto us," she whispered to Yanis during a meeting. "We need to accelerate our plan before they dismantle everything."

Yanis' eyes narrowed. "Proceed with phase two. Let's see how they handle this escalation."

As Monique implemented the next phase, unexpected resistance emerged. The IT team had managed to infiltrate their network, deploying countermeasures disrupting Monique's efforts. Their software began sending misleading data, causing confusion and delays.

In the midst of the digital battle, Cohen received an urgent call from a trusted source. "They're trying to escalate," the voice on the other end warned. "We need to stay a step ahead."

Cohen relayed the information to Garcia and Sheikh Wahhabi. "We must be proactive. Let's gather our allies and prepare for a coordinated response."

In the urban sprawl of Los Angeles, the IT team coordinated with activists and community leaders, ensuring the original message of the five-dollar project was spread through word-of-mouth and grassroots efforts. Social media campaigns were launched, emphasizing the power of unity and kindness, countering the narrative of control and manipulation.

Evelyn and Liam worked to gather testimonies and evidence, preparing a comprehensive report to expose the plans of Rayan and his associates. The exposé was published, causing a ripple of outrage and solidarity among the global participants.

Public outcry grew, and the movement regained its momentum. People across different cultures and continents reaffirmed their commitment to the original spirit of the five-dollar project. The message was clear: kindness could not be commandeered by those with ulterior motives.

In a final act of defiance, the IT team managed to shut down the primary servers controlling Rayan's software, crippling their operation. Realizing their plans were unraveling, Monique made a hasty retreat, but not before gathering crucial data implicating her superiors. Working to stop the movement had left Monique not liking trying to stop something good. She had learned about the movement for good and the people involved. She could see how happy they were and how working with Ryan's group kept her always unhappy. She decided to defect and work for good.

Now more vigilant than ever, the global community fortified their networks against future threats. Garcia, Cohen, and Sheikh Wahhabi's leadership inspired countless others to take up the mantle of kindness, ensuring the movement's resilience.

In a dimly lit room, Rayan Ysebaert, undeterred by the setbacks, stared at the flickering screens. "They may have won this round," he murmured to himself, "but the game is far from finished." His mind churned with new strategies, unwilling to concede defeat.

Yet, the world, having faced and overcome the manipulation, stood united in its resolve. The five-dollar movement, though tested, emerged stronger, a beacon of hope in an increasingly interconnected world.

In the midst of the urban rush, a sense of collective purpose simmered beneath the surface. People were mobilized, aware of the looming threats but galvanized by a shared commitment to the original cause.

In Evelyn's small apartment, a diverse group of allies gathered around a makeshift command center. Monique, having switched sides after recognizing the depth of Rayan's corruption, now sat among them, offering insights into his operation. The IT team was finalizing their plans to dismantle the remaining vestiges of the malicious software.

"We need to strike tonight," the IT team leader said, his eyes focused on the glowing screen. "Rayan won't expect a counterattack so soon. If we time it right, we can cripple their entire network."

Monique nodded, her expression determined. "I've already sent a decoy message to Yanis. They'll think we're still trying to patch the glitches. That should buy us enough time."

Meanwhile, Garcia and Cohen were in a secure video call with Sheikh Wahhabi. "Our contacts in various regions are ready," Garcia reported. "Community leaders are prepared to counter any misinformation and reinforce the true message of the five-dollar project."

Sheikh Wahhabi's voice was calm but resolute. "We must ensure our communication channels are secure. Any breach could undermine our efforts. Let's coordinate our final moves."

Rayan Ysebaert was already planning his next move in an underground bunker. His trusted lieutenants—Sacha, Yanis, Jules, and Martine—were gathered around a holographic display, detailing their remaining assets and strategies.

"We've lost significant ground," Sacha admitted, "but our core operations are intact. We can still pivot."

Rayan's eyes narrowed. "We need to regain control of the narrative. Use our media assets to create confusion. Spread rumors the five-dollar movement is a front for a larger conspiracy. Sow distrust among their ranks."

Yanis interjected, "Monique's betrayal has weakened our internal security. We need to be cautious. She knows too much about our infrastructure."

Rayan waved off the concern. "She's a minor setback. Focus on the bigger picture. If we can fracture their unity, we can reclaim the initiative."

As night fell, the IT team launched their coordinated cyber assault. The first wave targeted the primary servers, flooding them with decoy data and rendering them unresponsive. Paula's expertise in cybersecurity proved invaluable as she navigated the intricate web of defenses.

At the same time, Liam's exposé gained traction online. Social media platforms buzzed with discussions and hashtags trending globally as people rallied to support the five-dollar project. Evelyn and other grassroots leaders utilized these platforms to amplify their message, ensuring it reached every corner of the globe.

In a surprising turn of events, Monique's insider information led to the discovery of a critical vulnerability in Rayan's system. "This could give us direct access to their command center," she explained, pointing to a schematic. "We can shut them down from the inside."

The IT team leader's eyes lit up. "Let's do it."

An unexpected obstacle emerged just as they were about to execute the final stage. Rayan had anticipated a direct attack and set up a sophisticated, virtually impenetrable firewall. The clock was ticking, and their window of opportunity was closing fast.

In a moment of desperation, Emily suggested a radical idea. "What if we use the five-dollar network itself? We've established trust with participants worldwide. If we can mobilize them to perform a synchronized action, it might overwhelm Rayan's defenses."

Paula nodded thoughtfully. "It's risky, but it could work. The sheer volume of activity might create enough noise to slip through the cracks."

Garcia, on the video call, endorsed the plan. "Let's put our faith in the people. They've carried this movement forward. They can protect it too."

Messages were sent out to all participants of the five-dollar project. They were asked to perform a simple task at the same exact time: log into the project's website and share a message of kindness. The response was overwhelming. From New York to Nairobi, Tokyo to Timbuktu, millions of people logged in simultaneously, creating a tidal wave of activity.

The influx of data overwhelmed Rayan's firewall, creating openings the IT team could exploit. They breached the command center's defenses, systematically dismantling the control nodes.

In the bunker, alarms blared as systems went offline. Rayan watched in disbelief as his carefully constructed network crumbled. "Impossible," he muttered, realizing he had underestimated the collective power of the people he sought to control.

Even as Rayan's plans unraveled, he refused to concede. "We still have contingency plans," he told his lieutenants. "Initiate them immediately."

But the world had changed. The solidarity among the global participants had fortified their resolve. The people were no longer just followers; they were active protectors of the movement they cherished.

In the final moments of the battle, Monique and the IT team launched a decisive strike, severing Rayan's last channels of control. The digital fortress once symbolizing his dominion fell, and with it, his grip on the movement.

Sheikh Wahhabi, Garcia, and Cohen received the news of their victory. They felt a sense of relief and of purpose. They had protected something precious, not just a project but a symbol of humanity's potential for kindness and unity.

The five-dollar project flourished in the aftermath, its message of kindness and generosity more resonant than ever. Communities worldwide embraced the movement, fostering connections and inspiring change. Evelyn continued her work at the Quick Stop, but now she was more than a clerk; she was a beacon of hope.

Garcia, Cohen, and Sheikh Wahhabi, their bond stronger than ever, remained stewards of the movement, guiding it with wisdom and compassion. The IT team became guardians of the digital realm, ensuring the spirit of the project remained untarnished.

And Rayan Ysebaert, though defeated, plotted in the shadows. But the world, having tasted the power of collective goodwill, was ready to stand against any future threats. The five-dollar bill, a simple gesture of kindness, had sparked a revolution continuing to ripple across the globe, proving in unity, there is strength.

———

CHAPTER SIXTEEN
COLLABORATION OF FAITHS

Early morning sun filtered through the stained-glass windows of St. Michael's Church, casting colorful patterns on the wooden pews. Father Charles sat in his modest office, contemplating the note and five-dollar bill he had received from Maria Garcia, a devoted elderly parishioner. His mind wandered to the Savior's teachings on kindness and the parable of the Good Samaritan. This simple act of generosity had ignited a spark within him.

"Kindness," Father Charles mused aloud, "is like the loaves and fishes. It multiplies." He felt a profound sense of purpose as he jotted down names of local religious leaders who might join him in this initiative: Reverend Timothy, Bishop Gregory, Rabbi Levi, Priest Julius, and Imam Ishmael.

Picking up the phone, he began to dial. "It's time for miracles," he thought, feeling a mix of anticipation and hope. Each call was met with enthusiasm and support. The community outreach effort was set in motion, and a plan was formed to encourage every person in each congregation to participate. The idea was simple: use five dollars to perform an act of kindness and see how it spreads.

The first meeting with the religious leaders was scheduled for the following week. Father Charles arrived early, the anticipation growing with each tick of the clock. Reverend Timothy was the first to arrive, a tall man with a gentle demeanor. He greeted Father Charles warmly, expressing his eagerness to be part of this initiative.

"I'm glad you're leading this effort," Reverend Timothy said. "I've always believed small acts of kindness can lead to significant changes."

Bishop Gregory, a middle-aged man with a kind face and a firm handshake, was next. He shared stories of how his congregation had already embraced a ministering initiative. "We've seen firsthand how powerful ministering to one another can be," he said. "I'm excited to see what we can achieve together."

Rabbi Levi and Priest Julius arrived together, deep in conversation about their recent collaborative efforts. Their presence brought a sense of unity and shared purpose. With his thoughtful eyes and quiet strength, Rabbi Levi spoke of the importance of community support. Priest Julius, whose passion for social justice was well-known, echoed these sentiments, emphasizing the need for practical solutions.

Imam Ishmael was the last to arrive, his serene presence bringing calm to the room. He shared insights from his faith, highlighting the universal principles of compassion and charity. The discussion was rich with ideas and plans, each leader bringing their unique perspective to the table.

Despite the camaraderie, there were underlying differences in religious doctrines and practices. The challenge was to find common ground and focus on the shared goal of spreading kindness. Father Charles emphasized unity instead of division.

"Kindness knows no bounds," Father Charles began, his voice steady and filled with conviction. "Each of our faiths teaches us to care for our neighbors. This initiative can be a testament to our unity in diversity, showing despite our different paths, our destination is the same—compassion and love for all."

The leaders nodded in agreement. Reverend Timothy proposed each congregation encourage their members to use a five-dollar bill to perform one-on-one acts of kindness. This small sum, he believed, could have a profound impact if used thoughtfully.

Rabbi Levi suggested sharing these one-on-one experiences at their next meeting to inspire others and track the initiative's impact. "By sharing our stories, we can understand the real difference we're making," he said, his eyes shining with excitement.

Bishop Gregory volunteered his church's facilities for a gathering where congregants could share their experiences of giving and receiving five dollars. "It's a way to bring people together and highlight the power of individual generosity," he explained.

Priest Julius and Imam Ishmael discussed organizing interfaith events where participants could share their experiences of giving and receiving five dollars. "This initiative is not just about giving money," Priest Julius said. "It's about building bridges and strengthening our community."

As the meeting progressed, the leaders outlined a detailed plan for the upcoming months. They agreed to hold monthly gatherings to share updates and celebrate their successes. The room buzzed with energy and optimism as each leader committed to specific actions.

Father Charles felt a profound sense of hope and gratitude. This diverse group, brought together by a shared vision, was ready to embark on a journey of compassion and kindness. "We are stronger together," he said, his voice filled with emotion. "Let's show the world what unity can achieve."

In the ensuing weeks, the initiative gained momentum. Congregants from all walks of life participated, each act of kindness sparked by a simple five-dollar bill. Stories of generosity and compassion spread throughout the community, creating a ripple effect reaching far beyond the town's borders.

Reverend Timothy' church encouraged members to participate in the five-dollar challenge, where individuals were inspired to use their five dollars for personal acts of kindness. One member, Sarah, decided to give her five dollars to a young single mother she saw struggling to buy groceries. The mother, grateful and touched, used the money to buy essential items for her child. This act of kindness provided immediate help and restored her faith in human generosity.

With its strong tradition of ministering, Bishop Gregory's church embraced the initiative wholeheartedly. One elderly woman, Edith, used her five dollars to pay for a young man's bus fare when he realized he had lost his wallet. The young man, moved by her generosity, later returned to the church to volunteer, wanting to give back to the community helping him in a moment of need.

Rabbi Levi's congregation took a personal approach, encouraging one-on-one connections. Ronald, a member of the synagogue, gave his five dollars to a teenager who couldn't afford lunch at school. The teenager, deeply moved, later approached Ronald to thank him and share how his act of kindness had inspired him to help others in small ways, creating a chain of giving.

Priest Julius' church focused on individual interactions. Mary, a single mother struggling to make ends meet, used her five dollars to buy a small gift for her elderly neighbor who lived alone. The neighbor, touched by the unexpected kindness, started sharing his life stories with Mary, forming a bond providing both with much-needed companionship and support.

Imam Ishmael's mosque emphasized the importance of charity and compassion. One young man, Ahmed, decided to use his five dollars to buy flowers for a hospital patient he had never met. The patient, battling loneliness and illness, was overjoyed by the gesture. Ahmed's simple act of kindness brightened the patient's day and inspired hospital staff and other visitors to perform their own acts of generosity.

The Five-Dollar initiative transformed the community, proving even the smallest acts of kindness could make a significant difference. Inspired by their leaders and guided by their faith, members of each congregation reached out one-on-one, creating a ripple effect of generosity and compassion. Father Charles watched with pride and humility as the initiative flourished. The spark ignited by Maria Garcia's simple act of generosity had grown into a blazing fire of compassion, lighting the way for others to follow. The journey had only just begun, and the possibilities were endless.

Through their combined efforts, the religious leaders and their congregations demonstrated people can achieve extraordinary things when they come together with a shared purpose. The Five-Dollar initiative was a testament to the power of kindness, unity, and the unwavering belief by working together, we can change the world.

———

CHAPTER SEVENTEEN
THE DAWN OF GLOBAL KINDNESS

The United Nations Secretary-General, António Ricardo Salazar, settled into his leather chair, the world's weight resting on his shoulders. His office, GA 200, directly behind the General Assembly Hall, was his sanctuary amidst the chaos. He always arrived early to enjoy the only peace and quiet time of the day in the building. It was his time to think. As happened each day, his secretary, Sheryl Conroy, brought him a cup of steaming black Bolivian coffee—a small tie to his homeland—and the day's mail. He was looking toward a day of dealing with wars and rumors of war: Israel v. Palestine, Russia v. Ukraine, Kyrgyzstan v. Tajikistan, and the Gang War in Haiti. He much preferred to put off thinking about war until after breakfast, and his long-time secretary well knew it.

Sheryl Conroy entered with her usual efficiency. She placed a steaming cup on his desk, accompanied by the day's mail. But today, there was something different. A single, sealed letter lay atop the pile.

"I suggest you open this first," Sheryl said with a warm smile, her eyes twinkling with a hint of mystery.

Salazar raised an eyebrow. "Something important, perhaps something I'll like?"

Sheryl chuckled. "Could be, Mr. Secretary-General. Maybe the 'committee' insisted it be at the top of the list today."

"The committee?" Salazar echoed, amused. "Meaning the Sheryl Conroy Special Committee?"

"Maybe, sir. But it would be best if you didn't knock it until you've read it," Sheryl replied playfully.

"Are you going to wait for an answer?"

"If you don't mind."

Salazar took the envelope, its glued edges crisp under his fingers. He carefully cut it open and began to read. Sheryl, leaning in slightly, read over his shoulder, the block letter printing standing out starkly against the white paper. Sheryl read the letter in a strong whisper; it was not the first time she had seen the material.

Here is a gift, Mr. Secretary-General. Please pass it along.

So far, 125,000 people across the world have done just that.

It is past time the United Nations, WHO, and every well-meaning organization and person on the planet should do the same. You have great power and influence, Mr. Secretary-General. We ask you to use it. Pleading has not worked; shouting and arguing have not worked; diplomacy has not worked; and war has failed. Too many people have died; too much national treasure has been wasted so poverty and inhumanity persist. Let us try something new!

Attached to the letter was a crisp, new five-dollar bill. Salazar placed it on his desk, contemplating its significance.

"This is too simplistic, too... Pollyannaish... too different. I might become a laughingstock if I even suggest it. I am most dubious," he muttered.

"Sir, if I may," Sheryl interjected gently, "you are so highly respected no one will laugh or scoff. I think they might buy it. It's worth a try. If it comes to nothing, you can blame me, your stupid and simplistic Christian secretary."

Salazar smiled at her sincerity. "Then, maybe we could start small and see how it goes."

"That has already been done, sir. It has been exceptionally well received by hundreds of thousands of people, rich and poor, powerful and weak. I say it works. Let's see what can happen with the big guns focused on this project. If it does work, we must admit there was a way to get the world to agree to do away with war.

"You ought to run for office, Sheryl. You are most convincing. I'll tell you what. You get the right people from the right organizations and countries together for a serious meeting in the Great Assembly Hall, and I will be willing to push it. As the Americans say, I hope you have not bitten off more than you can chew."

Days later, the Great Assembly Hall buzzed with a sense of anticipation. Delegates from all corners of the globe filled the seats, their faces reflecting a mix of curiosity and skepticism. Salazar stood at the podium, the five-dollar bill prominently displayed in a clear acrylic case beside him.

"Ladies and gentlemen," he began, his voice resonating through the hall, "we gather here today not to discuss war nor to negotiate peace treaties. We are here to explore a new approach to fostering global unity and compassion—through the power of a single act of kindness."

He paused, allowing the weight of his words to settle.

The delegates exchanged excited glances, whispering amongst themselves, their faces alight with enthusiasm.

"As you all know," he continued, "this simple five-dollar bill represents a movement already touching the lives of more than 125,000 individuals worldwide. It symbolizes generosity and the ripple effect even the smallest acts of kindness can create."

Salazar recounted stories of individuals who had received and passed on a five-dollar bill, their lives changed by the chain of kindness. He spoke of Evelyn, the Quick Stop clerk, who gave the five-dollar bill to a needy customer and how it had sparked a series of generous deeds across her community.

Salazar continued seamlessly blending anecdotes from various authors who had contributed to the movement. Each story, a testament to the universal power of kindness, was met with murmurs of agreement and nods of approval.

He described how some had tried to exploit the movement for personal gain, only to be thwarted by the overwhelming response of genuine compassion from the global community. The IT team's counterattack against Rayan Ysebaert's manipulation efforts highlighted the resilience and unity emerging from the movement.

Salazar's voice softened as he concluded. "We have tried diplomacy, we have tried negotiation, and we have even tried war. None have brought us lasting peace. Let us now try kindness. Let us see what happens when we use our power and influence to foster a world where generosity and compassion are the norms rather than the exceptions."

The hall erupted in applause, the delegates rising to their feet in a standing ovation. Watching from the sidelines, Sheryl felt a swell of pride and hope.

Not everyone was convinced. Among the delegates sat the Russian delegate, Viktor Petrov. With his stern expression and meticulous attire, Petrov embodied the skepticism lingering in the minds of many. After the applause died down, he requested the floor.

"Mr. Secretary-General," Petrov began, his voice tinged with cynicism, "while I appreciate the sentiment behind this initiative, I must question its practicality. We live in a world governed by complex geopolitical interests and economic realities. Can we truly expect a five-dollar bill to bring about the change decades of diplomacy have failed to achieve?"

A murmur of agreement rippled through a section of the hall. Salazar remained composed, acknowledging Petrov's concerns.

"Mr. Petrov, your points are valid," Salazar replied calmly. "However, this initiative is not about replacing traditional diplomacy or economic strategies. It is about complementing them with a grassroots movement fostering a culture of kindness and empathy. It is about starting small and building a foundation upon which larger changes can be made."

Petrov remained unconvinced. "And what of those who seek to exploit this movement for their gain? How can we ensure the integrity of such a widespread initiative?"

Before Salazar could respond, Sheryl, who had been silently observing, stepped forward. "May I address that?" she asked, her voice steady.

Salazar nodded, allowing her to speak.

"Mr. Petrov, the beauty of this movement lies in its simplicity and the human connection it fosters. Yes, there will always be those who try to exploit it, but the overwhelming response of genuine kindness and the checks and balances we implement will help mitigate such risks. Moreover, the very nature of this initiative empowers individuals at the grassroots level, making it difficult for any one entity to control or manipulate it on a large scale."

Petrov eyed her with a mix of respect and skepticism. "It remains to be seen whether this idealism can withstand the harsh realities of our world. But for now, I will reserve judgment."

With that, the tension in the room eased, but the underlying conflict persisted. The challenge was to prove a simple act of kindness could ripple outward and create meaningful change in a world fraught with complexities.

Following the meeting, the movement gained unprecedented momentum. Governments, NGOs, and private organizations began incorporating the five-dollar initiative into their programs. Schools introduced Kindness Days, where students performed acts of kindness for their peers and communities. Corporations matched donations and encouraged employees to participate in volunteer activities.

In a small village in Kenya, a young girl named Amina received a five-dollar bill from a visiting aid worker. Inspired, she used the money to buy seeds, starting a community garden providing food for her entire village. Her story was shared globally, inspiring other communities to start similar projects.

In New York, a struggling artist named David found a five-dollar bill taped to his apartment door with a note: "Use this to create something beautiful." The gesture moved him, who had been on the verge of giving up his art. Instead, used the money to buy paint and canvases, creating a series of artworks depicting the power of kindness. His work gained national attention, leading to exhibitions and renewed hope for his career.

News outlets reported how the five-dollar bill had transformed lives, from funding small business ventures to paying for medical treatments.

In one instance, a group of high school students in Tokyo decided to pool their five-dollar bills to help a local orphanage. Their efforts improved the lives of the children and brought their community closer together, showcasing the far-reaching impact of collective generosity.

However, the movement faced significant hurdles. Carlos Sanchez, a corrupt politician, saw an opportunity to exploit the movement for personal gain. Sanchez began collecting five-dollar bills under the pretense of distributing them to the needy but instead used the funds personally. When the community discovered his deceit, outrage ensued. Protesters gathered outside his office, demanding accountability.

Grant Walter, a seasoned journalist, stepped forward. Driven by a passion for justice and patriotism and inspired by the stories of kindness he had reported on, Grant began an investigation into Sanchez's activities. His pursuit of the truth and the community's support led to Sanchez's eventual downfall. The scandal was a stark reminder of the potential for exploitation and highlighted the power of collective action and transparency.

In the wake of the scandal, the community rallied together, determined to restore the integrity of the movement. They introduced measures to ensure transparency and accountability, such as creating a publicly accessible ledger to track the distribution and impact of the five-dollar bills. These measures restored trust and strengthened the movement, demonstrating its resilience in the face of adversity.

The United Nations continued to champion the initiative, with Secretary-General Salazar leading by example. At a special session of the General Assembly, he presented a resolution to recognize and support the global kindness movement formally. The resolution passed unanimously, marking a historic moment in the organization's history.

Kindness spread far and wide as the world embraced this new approach to fostering peace and unity. Communities thrived, relationships strengthened, and the collective spirit of humanity shone brighter than ever.

Ultimately, it was not the grand gestures or the lofty speeches making the most significant impact. The simple, heartfelt acts of kindness—one five-dollar bill at a time—transformed the world.

———

Chapter Eighteen
The Seeds of Kindness

The concept of the five-dollar initiative was catching on in unexpected places. In a luxurious office filled with marble, ivory, and gold, a religious chief learned about the initiative's success from his assistant Jonas. "We should be doing the same," the chief said, his eyes gleaming with a mix of ambition and opportunism. "Hint on social media the idea came from us. It must be one of our followers who started it, so it won't be a lie."

Jonas, always eager to please, rubbed his hands together and smiled deviously. "No one does charity better than us. This is going to be fun." Orders were sent to the religious chief's generals and ten kings worldwide to get their congregations involved immediately.

Some of the religious chief's followers saw through the facade and voiced their concerns. "This isn't about genuine kindness," they argued. "It's about power and control." Tensions rose as the community became divided, with some supporting the initiative for its potential benefits and others wary of the chief's true intentions.

In a meeting with his generals, the religious chief outlined his plan. "We need to control the narrative," he said. "Make sure the public believes this was our idea from the start."

One of the generals, a pragmatic man named Khalid, raised a concern. "What if people see through it? This could backfire."

The chief waved off the concern. "We'll manage. Just focus on the positive outcomes. People love a good story of redemption and charity."

On the other side of the globe, a small group of believers gathered in a humble home. They knelt in prayer, seeking Ruach's guidance on participating in the five-dollar initiative. Despite their own poverty, they felt a deep calling to help others. The missionaries who served them were informed of their decision and spread the news to their head office. The head office, inspired by this act of faith, mailed out a thousand envelopes containing five-dollar bills and notes of blessing to communities around the world.

The missionaries faced logistical issues and skepticism from those they aimed to help. "What difference can five dollars make?" some questioned. "This won't change our circumstances." The missionaries had to work hard to gain the trust of the communities, showing small acts of kindness could indeed lead to larger changes.

Jonas executed the religious chief's orders with ruthless efficiency. The social media campaign was a success, and congregations around the world were mobilizing. However, the initiative took on a life of its own, transcending the chief's original intent. Genuine acts of kindness began to emerge, overshadowing the initial opportunism.

But this success also attracted unwanted attention. Critics accused the religious chief of using the initiative for self-promotion and financial gain. "This is just a publicity stunt," they claimed. The chief had to navigate these accusations carefully, balancing the need for transparency with the desire to maintain his influence.

In a press conference, the religious chief addressed the concerns.

"This initiative is about spreading kindness and helping those in need," he said. "While we may have started it, the true credit goes to the countless individuals who have embraced it with genuine hearts."

Despite the criticism, the initiative continued to grow. Stories of kindness and generosity flooded social media, inspiring people around the world to participate. The chief's initial intentions were overshadowed by the movement's genuine impact.

In the missionary head office, administrators marveled at the generosity and enthusiasm spread globally. Reports flooded in from communities where the five-dollar bills had sparked movements of compassion and support. The initiative had indeed lifted the poor out of despair, proving kindness and generosity were powerful tools for change.

But challenges remained. Logistical issues, cultural differences, and the sheer scale of the initiative required constant attention and adaptation. The administrators worked tirelessly, motivated by the belief their efforts were making a real difference.

One major logistical challenge was ensuring the five-dollar bills reached the intended recipients. In some regions, postal systems were unreliable, and there was a risk of the money being intercepted. The administrators partnered with local organizations to distribute the bills directly, ensuring they reached those in need.

In addition to logistical challenges, cultural differences sometimes created misunderstandings. In one community, a well-intentioned act of kindness was misinterpreted as a form of charity, causing offense. The administrators quickly stepped in to mediate, emphasizing the spirit of mutual respect and understanding underpinned the initiative.

Despite these challenges, the initiative continued to grow. The five-dollar bills became symbols of hope and connection, transcending cultural and geographical boundaries.

Seeds of kindness had been sown, and the world was beginning to see the fruits of this collective effort. The five-dollar bills continued to circulate, each one a beacon of hope and a reminder of the profound impact small acts of kindness could have on individuals and communities alike.

The spirit of generosity ignited by a single five-dollar bill had grown into a global movement, uniting people from all walks of life in a shared mission to spread kindness and compassion.

Amidst the widespread goodwill, challenges and conflicts continued to arise as some sought to exploit the initiative for personal gain. Yet, the enduring power of genuine acts of kindness prevailed, demonstrating the human spirit's capacity for empathy and generosity could shine through even in the face of adversity.

———

CHAPTER NINETEEN
BEHIND BARS

Jack, who had once been at rock bottom, was now a zealous advocate for the Five Dollar program. He had experienced firsthand how a single five-dollar bill could change a life. Once an alcoholic and criminal, Jack had found redemption through this simple act of kindness. Now, he was determined to introduce the program into prisons and reformatories, believing even those who had strayed far could find a path back through small acts of generosity.

Jack decided to start by connecting with people living on the streets and then move on to the local jail. He knew when someone at the bottom reached out to help another, it brought them a step closer to wanting to improve their own life. This newfound purpose gave Jack a sense of fulfillment and contentment he had never known.

Local authorities were skeptical about his intentions, considering his criminal past. "Why should we trust him?" they questioned. "What if this is just another scheme?" Jack had to prove his sincerity, not just through words but through consistent actions. It was an uphill battle, but

Jack was determined to show people could change—that he had changed.

One evening, Jack stood at the entrance of a homeless shelter, clutching a stack of five-dollar bills. He had spent weeks trying to gain permission to distribute them here, facing bureaucratic hurdles and skepticism. The shelter director, a stern woman named Ms. Lopez, had finally given him a chance, albeit reluctantly.

"Let's see if your actions speak louder than your words," she had said.

Jack handed out the bills and a simple note: "This is for you. Pass it on." The reactions were mixed—some grateful, others suspicious. One man, a former soldier, looked at Jack with piercing eyes.

"What's your angle?" he asked, his voice rough with distrust.

"No angle," Jack replied calmly. "Just trying to spread a little kindness."

He pocketed the bill, his expression softening. "We'll see," he muttered, walking away.

Another time, in a prison on the outskirts of the city, Jack stood before a group of inmates. He shared his own story of redemption, encouraging them to participate in the Five Dollar program. The men listened intently, some with skepticism, others with a glimmer of hope. Jack's sincerity and passion were palpable, and as he handed out five-dollar bills, he saw the beginnings of a transformation in their eyes.

Some inmates scoffed at the idea, entrenched in their cynicism. "This won't change anything," they sneered. Jack faced an uphill battle to convince them otherwise. He knew true change would take time and persistence.

One of the most vocal skeptics was a man named Tony, a hardened criminal with a reputation for trouble. "You're wasting your time, Jack," Tony said. "People like us don't change."

"I used to think the same way. But I've seen the difference it can make. Just give it a chance."

For the next few weeks, Jack worked closely with the inmates, sharing stories of hope and redemption. Slowly, he began to see changes. Some men started participating in small acts of kindness within the prison, helping each other in ways they hadn't before.

Tony remained resistant, but a breakthrough came during a group session one evening. Jack had asked the inmates to share something positive they had done recently.

"I helped a guy in my cell block," Tony said reluctantly. "He was having a rough time, and I gave him some of my commissary."

The room fell silent, then erupted in applause. Jack smiled, knowing this was just the beginning.

———

CHAPTER TWENTY
KINDNESS WITHOUT STRINGS

Evelyn hurried to her shift at the Quick Stop. Her mind was preoccupied with thoughts of the five-dollar bill she had passed on to a struggling customer. The memory of the woman's grateful expression made her smile. Evelyn had shared the story with her daughter, Amy, and they had decided to become agents of kindness in their neighborhood. They started small, helping their elderly neighbor, Mrs. Jackson, by buying groceries and leaving them anonymously at her door.

Their actions sparked a quiet wave of kindness among their neighbors. Inspired by Evelyn and Amy's secret missions, the community began to look out for one another. Small acts of generosity became commonplace, weaving a new fabric of connection and support. The once-ordinary neighborhood transformed into a place where kindness was the norm, and people began to take notice of the positive changes around them.

Some neighbors questioned their motives, suspicious of their sudden acts of generosity. "What's in it for them?" they whispered. Evelyn and Amy faced criticism and doubt but continued their mission undeterred, believing in the power of kindness to overcome skepticism. They knew generosity often encountered resistance, but they had faith their consistent efforts would ultimately convince the skeptics.

One afternoon, as Evelyn and Amy were planting flowers in Mrs. Jackson's garden, a neighbor, Mr. Thompson, approached them. His stern face and crossed arms conveyed his skepticism. He had been watching their activities with a critical eye, unsure of their intentions.

"What are you really up to?" he asked bluntly. "People don't just do things for others without expecting something in return." His tone was accusatory, and his gaze intense, as if trying to uncover a hidden agenda.

Evelyn stood up, wiped her hands on her jeans and looked Mr. Thompson in the eye, her expression calm and sincere. "We're just trying to make our neighborhood a better place," she said calmly. "No strings attached." Her voice was steady, filled with conviction and genuine kindness.

Mr. Thompson's eyes narrowed as he scrutinized Evelyn and Amy. "We'll see," he muttered, turning away. Despite his harsh words, there was a flicker of curiosity in his eyes. The seed of doubt had been planted, but so had a seed of hope. Perhaps, he thought, there was something genuine in their actions after all.

Days turned into weeks, and Evelyn and Amy's efforts continued. They organized a neighborhood cleanup, gathered donations for the local food bank, and even set up a small free library on their street. Their enthusiasm was infectious, slowly breaking down the walls of skepticism and mistrust initially greeting their acts of kindness.

One morning, Mr. Thompson found a basket of freshly baked cookies on his doorstep, with a note reading, "Just a little something to brighten your day." It was signed, "Your neighbors, Evelyn and Amy." He stared at the basket for a long moment, the aroma of the cookies wafting up to him, stirring something deep within his heart.

He picked up a cookie and took a bite. It was delicious. He couldn't help but smile, a small but significant crack in his hardened exterior.

One morning, Mr. Thompson found a five-dollar bill taped to his door with a note reading, "Use this to make someone smile today. - Your neighbors, Evelyn and Amy." He stared at the bill and the note for a long moment, the simple message stirring something deep within his heart.

He pocketed the bill and decided to use it at the local coffee shop. He bought a coffee for the person behind him in line, a young woman who looked tired and stressed. Her surprised smile and heartfelt thanks warmed his heart, and he realized how powerful even a small act of kindness could be.

One evening, Mr. Thompson walked to Evelyn and Amy's house. They were sitting on the porch, enjoying the cool breeze. He hesitated for a moment, then cleared his throat.

"I owe you an apology," he said, his voice gruff but sincere. "I was wrong to doubt your intentions. You've shown me kindness doesn't need a reason. It just needs a heart."

Evelyn smiled warmly, and Amy jumped up to give him a hug. "It's never too late to join us," she said. "Together, we can make an even bigger difference."

From that day on, he became an active participant in their mission, spreading kindness in every way he could. The neighborhood continued to thrive, a testament to the power of small acts of generosity and the courage to believe in the goodness of others. Evelyn's simple act of giving a five-dollar bill sparked a chain reaction, proving even the smallest gestures could have a profound impact.

———

CHAPTER TWENTY-ONE
THE RIPPLE'S CREST

The world was alive with the energy of transformation. From bustling metropolises to quiet, remote villages, the story of a single five-dollar bill had woven a web of human connection, resilience, and boundless generosity. It was a movement transcending borders and bridged divides, a living testament to the power of a small act of kindness.

A diverse group of individuals gathered in a grand hall in New York City. This was not just any meeting; it was a global summit dedicated to the Five Dollar Initiative. Here, the key figures whose lives had intertwined with the journey of the five-dollar bill came together to share their stories, reflect on their experiences, and chart the future of this extraordinary movement.

At the front of the hall, a large stage was set up, flanked by screens displaying images and videos from the journey of the five-dollar bill. The atmosphere was electric with anticipation as people from all walks of life filled the seats, their faces glowing with hope and inspiration.

Jerry Bleven, the man whose act of generosity had ignited this global movement, stood backstage, reflecting on the journey bringing him here. His mind drifted to the day he lost his job. The stark reality of financial insecurity had loomed large, but his wife Clara's unwavering support had been his anchor. The memory of their resolve to shield their children from the harshness of their situation was still vivid. He remembered when he had handed his last five dollars to Evelyn, the Quick Stop clerk. Little did he know this simple act would set off a chain reaction of kindness reaching far beyond his wildest dreams.

Clara's belief in the power of kindness had been a beacon of hope during those dark days.

Evelyn, who had received Jerry's five-dollar bill, stood beside him. Her journey from a Quick Stop clerk to an ambassador of kindness had been nothing short of miraculous. She recalled the young woman who had entered the store, unable to afford her groceries. Evelyn's decision to pass on Jerry's five-dollar bill had helped her and set in motion a wave of goodwill touching countless lives.

As Jerry and Evelyn prepared to step onto the stage, their thoughts were interrupted by the arrival of Maria Innocenta Garcia. Maria's once quiet life had been transformed by the five-dollar bill she received. It had rekindled a sense of purpose in her, leading her to spread joy and kindness within her community. Maria's story was a poignant reminder of how even the smallest gestures could breathe new life into the most unexpected places.

The three of them shared a moment of quiet reflection before stepping onto the stage. The audience erupted into applause, their faces alight with admiration and gratitude. Jerry, Evelyn, and Maria took their seats, and the room fell silent as the lights dimmed and a video began to play.

The screens lit up with the title Five Dollars: A Ripple of Change, and the documentary began. It was a powerful narrative tracing the journey of the five-dollar bill, from Jerry's initial act of kindness to the countless lives it had touched. The audience watched in awe as the stories of Sandy, Jack, Anna, Hyrum, and many others unfolded before their eyes.

The documentary highlighted the pivotal moments in each person's journey. Inspired by the five-dollar bill, Sandy's decision to leave her partner and start anew had led her to create a community garden which became a sanctuary for many. Jack's transformation from a life of crime to an artist who used his talent to inspire others was a testament to the redemptive power of kindness. Anna's Five Dollar Day initiative had revolutionized her community, demonstrating how small acts of generosity could create a ripple effect of positive change.

Hyrum R. Patterson's corporate philanthropy had given the initiative a powerful platform, turning it into a national movement. His belief in the collective power of kindness had inspired countless individuals to pay it forward. The documentary also showcased the global impact of the initiative, with stories of generosity from around the world, from the bustling streets of Tokyo to the serene landscapes of rural Africa.

As the documentary concluded, the audience sat in reflective silence, moved by the profound impact of the five-dollar bill. The lights came back on, and Jerry, Evelyn, and Maria stood to address the crowd.

"Thank you all for being here today," Jerry began, his voice steady and filled with emotion. "What started as a simple act has grown into something beyond our wildest dreams. We've seen how a single five-dollar bill can transform lives, create communities, and inspire a global movement."

Evelyn stepped forward, her eyes shining with pride. "This journey has shown kindness knows no bounds. It transcends cultures, languages, and borders. It's a universal language connecting us all."

Maria, her voice soft but firm, added, "At 94, I thought my days of making a difference were passed. But this five-dollar bill gave me a new purpose. It reminded me it's never too late to spread joy and kindness."

The crowd erupted into applause once more as the three of them took their seats. The summit continued with speakers from around the world sharing their experiences and insights. Leaders of various organizations, community activists, and ordinary individuals who had been inspired by the initiative took to the stage, each story adding a new layer to the composition of kindness.

One of the most poignant moments came when a young woman named Leah shared her story. She had been a victim of domestic abuse and had found refuge in a shelter where she received a five-dollar bill giving her the strength to rebuild her life. Today, Leah runs a non-profit organization supporting survivors of domestic violence, and her story is a powerful testament to the enduring impact of kindness.

As inspiring as the summit was, it was also a time to acknowledge the struggles and conflicts arising along the way. Hyrum R. Patterson took the stage to share his experience of implementing the initiative within his corporation. Initially, his vision of using the company's resources to foster kindness was met with skepticism and resistance from the board of directors. Many feared such a radical shift would harm their profits and destabilize the company's market position.

"I faced a lot of pushback," Hyrum admitted to the audience. "But I knew the potential for positive change outweighed the risks. It wasn't easy convincing everyone, but through persistence and the visible impact of our pilot programs, we began to see a shift in attitude. It wasn't just about the money; it was about changing the culture of our organization."

Hyrum's struggle highlighted a critical aspect of the initiative: the importance of perseverance in the face of opposition. His story resonated with many in the audience who had faced similar challenges in their own efforts to spread kindness.

In another part of the world, the initiative had sparked both hope and tension. In a tent in the Middle East, Sheikh Mohammad Abu Baker al-Saud Wahhabi and his friends, Maria Innocenta Garcia and Abraham ben Cohen, had embraced the initiative wholeheartedly. Their efforts to promote interfaith harmony through acts of kindness were met with both enthusiasm and resistance.

Sheikh Mohammad recounted an incident in which a militant faction viewed their efforts as a threat to their control. "They saw our message of unity and kindness as a challenge to their power," he explained. "We faced threats and intimidation, but we stood our ground, believing in the power of our mission."

The tension escalated to a point where their lives were at risk. However, through their unwavering commitment and the support of their community, they managed to turn the tide. The conflict ultimately strengthened their resolve and brought their community closer together.

Jack's journey of redemption was fraught with conflict. After leaving his criminal past behind, he faced significant obstacles in his quest to spread kindness within the prison system. Initially met with cynicism and hostility from both inmates and authorities, Jack's persistence eventually won the hearts of many.

"There were days when I wanted to give up," Jack confessed to the summit attendees. "The resistance was overwhelming, and it felt like an uphill battle. But every small victory, every inmate who chose to pay it forward, reminded me why I started this journey."

Jack's story underscored the importance of resilience and the transformative power of kindness, even in the most challenging environments. His efforts had sparked a movement of compassion and redemption within the prison, proving no one was beyond the reach of kindness.

As the summit continued, it became clear the five-dollar initiative had inspired acts of kindness and faced significant challenges. The spread of the initiative had attracted the attention of individuals and groups with nefarious intentions. There were instances where people attempted to exploit the movement for personal gain, undermining its core values.

Journalist Grant Walters shared his investigation into a scandal involving a corrupt politician, Carlos Sanchez, who had tried to hijack the initiative for his own benefit. "Sanchez saw the initiative as a way to gain political leverage," Grant explained. "He manipulated the system to funnel funds into his campaign, betraying the very principles of the movement."

The revelation of Sanchez's corruption had caused a temporary setback, casting a shadow over the initiative. However, the collective efforts of the community, coupled with Grant's relentless pursuit of the truth, exposed Sanchez's deceit and restored the movement's integrity.

Yet, not all conflicts were resolved so cleanly. As the movement grew, so did the resistance from those who felt threatened by the change it represented. In various parts of the world, the initiative encountered pushback ranging from skepticism to outright hostility.

In a small town in the American Midwest, the five-dollar initiative faced a particularly virulent backlash. It began with murmurs of discontent among the townsfolk, who saw the movement as a threat to their traditional way of life. These murmurs soon grew into snide remarks and mockery.

"Look at the do-gooders. What do they think they are doing? It's all meaningless," some would sneer as they passed by the local community center where volunteers gathered to plan acts of kindness. The situation escalated when a group of dissenters began organizing protests. They carried signs and shouted slogans questioning the integrity and motives of the movement's participants. One day, the protests turned violent. What started as a peaceful demonstration quickly devolved into chaos as tempers flared and shoving matches broke out. The tension reached a tragic climax when an elderly man, beloved in the community for his steadfast support of the initiative, was struck and killed by a car during the pandemonium. The driver, blinded by rage and confusion, had not intended to cause harm, but the consequences were irrevocable.

The entire town was stunned. The death of the old man, who had been a symbol of the movement's gentle spirit, enveloped the community in grief. For the first time, the people involved in the five-dollar initiative faced the stark reality their efforts, however noble, could provoke profound anger and violence.

The community was subdued by the realization their efforts at spreading kindness had been met with such vicious opposition. The shock of what had happened spurred the group to reflect deeply on their mission and its implications. They faced a critical juncture: How should they respond to such overt hatred and violence?

The leaders of the initiative, including Jerry, Evelyn, and Maria, gathered to discuss the way forward. They decided to address the tragedy with the same spirit of kindness and compassion defining their movement from the beginning. They reached out to the driver who had accidentally caused the death of their friend. Rather than seeking retribution, they offered forgiveness and support.

"We must remember why we started this journey," Jerry said during a community meeting. "We wanted to make the world a better place, to spread kindness and compassion. Our mission doesn't change because we've encountered resistance. If anything, it makes our resolve even stronger."

Evelyn wrote a heartfelt editorial for the local newspaper, explaining why it was important to care about total strangers and the profound impact of small acts of kindness. Her words struck a chord with many, rekindling the flame of hope and generosity in the hearts of those who had started to waver.

Maria, drawing on her long life of wisdom, gave a moving speech at a town hall meeting. "There will always be those who oppose change, who fear the light kindness brings. But we must stand firm. Love always has power over evil. We cannot eliminate all the darkness in the world, but we can shine our light brightly and make a difference."

The town began to heal. The violent protest had shaken the community, but it also galvanized the supporters of the initiative. They redoubled their efforts, reaching out to those who had been injured and providing support to the grieving family of the old man who had been killed. Their actions spoke louder than any words, demonstrating the true power of forgiveness and compassion.

In the following weeks, the five-dollar initiative saw a resurgence of support. The community, once divided, began to come together in a new spirit of unity and cooperation. The tragic event had underscored a critical lesson: even in the face of hatred and violence, love and kindness could prevail.

As the summit attendees shared their stories of struggle and triumph, it became clear the five-dollar initiative had inspired acts of kindness and taught valuable lessons about resilience and the human spirit. The closing ceremony was a powerful testament to these lessons.

Jerry, Evelyn, and Maria were joined on stage by other key figures of the initiative, including Hyrum, Jack, and Leah. Each of them was given an opportunity to share their final thoughts and reflections.

Jerry began, his voice resonating with emotion. "Today, we stand together as a testament to the power of kindness. What started as a simple act has grown into a global movement touching countless lives. We have faced challenges and overcome obstacles, but through it all, we have remained united in our commitment to making the world a better place."

Evelyn followed, her words filled with pride and hope. "This journey has shown us kindness knows no bounds. It is a universal language connecting us all. We have seen the incredible impact of small acts of generosity, and we know this is only the beginning."

Maria, her voice filled with wisdom and grace, added, "At 94, I never imagined I could still make a difference. But this five-dollar bill has shown me spreading joy and kindness is never too late. It has given me a renewed sense of purpose, and I am grateful to be a part of this journey."

Hyrum, reflecting on his corporate experience, emphasized the importance of resilience and perseverance. "We faced skepticism and resistance but stayed true to our vision. The impact of our efforts has been profound, and we have shown kindness can thrive even in the most challenging environments."

With a deep sense of redemption, Jack spoke about his journey from darkness to light. "I have seen firsthand the transformative power of kindness. It has given me a second chance, and I am committed to paying it forward. We must continue to spread this message and inspire others to join us."

Leah, representing the new generation of leaders inspired by the initiative, shared her vision for the future. "We have the power to create a brighter, more compassionate world. The five-dollar bill has shown us even the smallest act of kindness can create ripples of change. Let us carry this legacy forward and continue to inspire others."

As the closing ceremony drew to a close, the audience rose to their feet in a standing ovation. The energy in the room was palpable, a reflection of the collective commitment to continue the work of the five-dollar initiative.

The final moments of the summit were marked by a symbolic gesture. Each attendee was given a five-dollar bill and a note encouraging them to perform an act of kindness. The bills were passed hand to hand, symbolizing the ongoing journey and the potential for positive change.

As the attendees left the grand hall, they carried a renewed sense of purpose and a commitment to spreading kindness in their communities. The five-dollar initiative had created a global network of individuals dedicated to making the world a better place, one small act at a time.

The story of the five-dollar bill was far from complete. It would continue to travel, touching lives and inspiring acts of kindness in ways that could never be fully measured. The legacy of the five-dollar bill lived on, a beacon of hope and a reminder even the smallest act of kindness could create ripples spreading across the world.

The journey had only just begun, and the possibilities were endless. Together, they had created something extraordinary—a global movement proving even the smallest act of kindness could change the world.

———

Epilogue: A Global Legacy of Kindness

The United Nations Department of Peace Operations had undergone a profound transformation in the past decade. Once solely focused on maintaining peace in conflict zones, it now championed a global initiative beginning with a simple act of kindness—a five-dollar bill passed from one person to another. This initiative, known as the Five Dollar Peace Initiative, had woven a web of generosity spanning the globe, transcending cultures, religions, and socioeconomic barriers.

In a world where peacekeepers often operated in fragile security conditions, the UN's training programs evolved to include materials focused on fostering kindness and anti-war principles. This was no ordinary mission. Peacekeepers were now greeted with celebrations instead of fear—Jewish children saw them as Purim-like festivities, American children enjoyed what felt like a second Fourth of July, Muslims celebrated with the joy of Eid al-Fitr, and people in India and Singapore compared it to the lights and joy of Diwali. It felt like a second Christmas in Europe, and in Russia, it was as if both New Years were celebrated together.

The Five Dollar Proclamation reached a distribution milestone, spreading kindness to 90 percent of the world's population. The initiative's success was undeniable, and there had been no new wars since its widespread adoption. People whispered about this miraculous peace, careful not to jinx the wondrous transformation.

The new Secretary-General, Safiatou Bakayoko, once the president of Côte d'Ivoire, was determined to celebrate this monumental success. Celebrations were planned at global venues, including the United Nations Plaza in New York City, Washington, D.C., Addis Ababa in Ethiopia, Montreal in Canada, Santo Domingo in the Dominican Republic, Macau in China, the United Nations University in Tokyo, Amman in Jordan, Bangkok in Thailand, the UN Regional Centre in Ashgabat, Turkmenistan, the United Nations International School in Hanoi, Copenhagen in Denmark, and Trieste in Italy. Applications to participate poured in from hundreds of other countries, eager to join the festivities.

Secretary-General Bakayoko tasked the UN intelligence services with identifying all the originators of the Five Dollar Peace Initiative. In an unprecedented show of trust, every UN nation granted carte blanche privileges to MPKIO officers to identify these pioneers. Hundreds of officers joined forces with local security forces, sifting through countless names to ensure credit was given where due.

The final list of honorees included a surprising array of individuals: Jerry Bleven, Evelyn Rodriguez, Sheikh Mohammad Abu Baker al-Saud Wahhabi, Maria Innocenta Garcia, Abraham ben Cohen, Hyrum R. Patterson, Giovanni Carpegna, the late former UN General Secretary

António Ricardo Salazar, Manny, and Anna, whose contributions had profoundly impacted the movement. These individuals were celebrated for spreading kindness and fostering global peace.

Jerry Bleven, Clara Bleven, Evelyn Rodriguez Zhang, Jack and Sandy Jones, Manny, Anna, and other key figures gathered for a celebratory dinner at the UN Plaza Grill in New York. Amid the sumptuous feast of prime dry-aged steaks, Japanese-inspired dishes, seafood, and sushi, stories of the past decade flowed like water.

Evelyn, never one for public speaking, nervously volunteered to go first. "I just want you guys to know everything has picked up for me. I met a great guy, Michael Zhang, whose wife had passed away. Jerry introduced us. Michael makes a good living, and I can be a stay-at-home mom like I always wanted. Besides my daughter, we have three of the cutest kids in the world—and the smartest, if you don't mind me bragging a little."

Jerry Bleven followed. "I had kind of a miracle. Someone gave five bucks to a sweet older lady who was very rich and wanted to do something good. She found out about me and got her son to give me a job, which put me in contact with people in New York who know all about stock and bond portfolios. My wife and I made a bundle, and we are putting our two kids through Harvard. By the way, they are all the way into the Five Dollar Peace Initiative. That little thing of giving five dollars is going gangbusters everywhere now!"

Manny, who had been listening attentively, shared his story next. "For me, it started with those two five-dollar bills I had left in my wallet. Inspired by a conversation at the homeless shelter, I decided to pass them on with a note. One went to Maria Innocenta Garcia, and the other went to Abraham Ben Cohen. Ten years later, I've gone from managing a delivery company to owning it. But the real joy has been in giving back—sending gifts of love, cheer, and flowers to people in healthcare facilities and nursing homes. Seeing their smiles and knowing I've brightened their day is the best reward."

Anna, sitting beside Manny, added her story to the mix. "George and I started Five Dollar Day at our hospital, where we worked to provide free prescriptions to those in need. This initiative didn't just stop at our hospital; it became a model for hospitals worldwide. Along the way, George and I went from being colleagues to friends to a married couple with four beautiful girls. Our family and our work have been deeply intertwined with this initiative."

Stories of transformation and triumph continued, each more heartwarming than the last. Finally, Giovanni Carpegna, now wheelchair-bound and on oxygen, shared his tale. "Look, youse, don't shed no tears for me. Lookit this swell suit I got on. I got an anonymous stock tip from an unknown person—a sweet girl named Evelyn." Laughter filled the room. "And I heard from a little birdie she married up with some real rich dude, got a passel of beautiful kids, and is a real success. I gotta say, I'm glad for me, and I'm real glad for her. We all come a long ways on nothin' but five bucks."

The five-dollar gift had morphed into a global movement, touching millions of lives. It had grown into five euros, five yen, five rupees—every currency imaginable. The magic of kindness became a universal language. People held their politicians accountable, insisted on honesty, and fostered communities built on caring and compassion. Governments balanced budgets and funded essential services like job training, affordable housing, and cancer research.

The five-dollar movement reshaped societies, proving small acts of kindness could spark significant change. Reminders that "Evil is forever—we can't rest on our laurels! Do something loving today." were posted everywhere, ensuring the spirit of the initiative endured.

Traditional charity organizations and large religious institutions saw a decline, replaced by small, close-knit communities where love and kindness were central. The movement's strength lay in its simplicity and the profound impact of genuine, personal connections.

Abraham ben Cohen sat in his office, reflecting on the past ten years. Maria Innocenta Garcia was gone, and Sheikh Mohammad was negotiating with world leaders. The phrase "five dollars" had become synonymous with kindness. Millions gave and received acts of kindness, proving small actions could change the world.

The Five Dollar Peace Initiative legacy was apparent as the celebrations continued worldwide. It had become a powerful force for good, uniting people across cultures and continents in a shared commitment to kindness. The world had been transformed, and the ripple effect of a single act of generosity continued to inspire hope, joy, and love.

The journey of the five-dollar bill showed when individuals come together with a shared purpose, they can create a brighter, more compassionate world. This story of interconnected lives and collective action is a testament to the enduring power of kindness and the remarkable impact of even the smallest gestures.

As the evening at the UN Plaza Grill continued, the group reflected on the extraordinary journey bringing them together. Each person's story was a testament to the transformative power of kindness. They had all faced challenges, yet passing a five-dollar bill had created a ripple effect changing countless lives.

Evelyn's story of meeting Michael Zhang and becoming a stay-at-home mom resonated deeply with Clara Bleven. She thought about her journey with Jerry and their challenges together. Clara shared how Jerry's job loss had initially seemed like an insurmountable obstacle, but it ultimately led them to new opportunities and a brighter future.

Jerry nodded in agreement, adding, "It's amazing how one small act can lead to so much change. When I gave five dollars to Evelyn, I had no idea it would come back to us. It shows you never know how far your kindness can go."

Giovanni Carpegna, despite his health challenges, had an air of resilience and humor. "Youse know, when I got that anonymous stock tip, I thought it was a joke. But it was the best thing that ever happened to me. And Evelyn, you're the reason behind it all. I owe you more than just a thank you."

Evelyn blushed, modestly deflecting the praise. "I just did what felt right. It was the kindness of so many others that made this possible." I also want to tell you something Michael told me about Jerry.

When Jerry worked for Michael, his nickname was Miracle Worker. Jerry sure created a miracle, bringing Michael and me together.

Sitting side by side, Jack and Sandy Jones shared their transformation tale. Jack's journey from despair to hope had been marked by significant struggles and moments of profound generosity and support. Sandy had played a crucial role in helping him find his path, and their reunion at the charity event had rekindled their bond.

"Sandy believed in me when I didn't believe in myself," Jack said, his voice filled with emotion. "And her belief helped me turn my life around. The Five Dollar Peace Initiative gave me a second chance."

Sandy squeezed his hand, her eyes reflecting the strength of their shared experiences. "We all deserve second chances, Jack. And this initiative has shown even the smallest acts of kindness can create opportunities for redemption and growth."

As the conversations flowed, it became clear the Five Dollar Peace Initiative had not only transformed individual lives but had also reshaped communities and nations. The initiative's influence had reached the highest government levels, inspiring policies prioritizing compassion and accountability.

Governments worldwide began implementing programs mirroring the Five Dollar Peace Initiative principles. They focused on reducing unnecessary spending, promoting job training, providing affordable housing, and investing in cancer research and other critical areas. Politicians who once thrived on divisiveness and power struggles found themselves held to higher standards by their constituents.

The initiative had also fostered a sense of global unity. People from diverse backgrounds and cultures came together with a shared purpose. They celebrated their differences while recognizing their common humanity. Thanks to the simple act of giving, the world has become more compassionate and connected.

As the evening drew to a close, the group reflected on the journey bringing them to this moment. They knew the work was far from finished. The world will always face challenges, and the need for kindness and compassion will remain constant.

But they were also filled with hope. They had seen firsthand the incredible impact small acts of kindness could have. They had witnessed the transformation of lives, communities, and nations. And they knew the legacy of the Five Dollar Peace Initiative would continue to inspire future generations.

Secretary-General Bakayoko's voice echoed in their minds as they left the UN Plaza Grill. "The Five Dollar Peace Initiative is more than just a movement. It is a testament to the power of human kindness and the potential for positive change. Let us continue to spread this message of hope and compassion and build a brighter, more peaceful world for all."

A week after the reunion at the UN Plaza Grill, Evelyn decided to reconnect with some of the people whose lives had been touched by the five-dollar bill. She reached out to Sandy, who now coordinated the community garden project, and the two arranged to meet.

At the community garden, Evelyn marveled at the lush greenery and vibrant flowers. Sandy greeted her with a warm hug and a tour of the garden. "This place has become a sanctuary for many," Sandy explained. "People come here not just to work but to find peace and connect with others."

Evelyn smiled. "It's beautiful, Sandy. You've created something extraordinary here."

They spent the afternoon sharing stories and reflecting on the journey bringing them to this point. Sandy introduced Evelyn to some of the garden's volunteers, including Ayesha, the librarian who had helped Sandy find her way.

The community garden was just one example of how the Five Dollar Peace Initiative had transformed local communities. In neighborhoods worldwide, people had come together to create spaces where kindness and compassion thrived.

For instance, in a small town in Italy, a group of volunteers started a Kindness Café, where patrons could pay for a coffee in advance for someone in need. The café became a hub of generosity, with customers often leaving notes of encouragement along with their pre-paid coffees. The owners expanded the concept, offering free meals and organizing community events bringing people together.

In Tokyo, a young woman started a Kindness Library inspired by the initiative. She collected books from donations and created a space where anyone could borrow or donate books. The library became a haven for those seeking knowledge and companionship, fostering a sense of community in the bustling city.

Jerry and Clara Bleven continued to support the initiative through their newfound wealth. They established a foundation funding educational programs, job training, and community projects. One of their proudest achievements was a scholarship program for students pursuing social work and community development careers.

Jerry often visited the schools and community centers supported by the foundation. During one such visit, he met a young man named Jude, who had received a scholarship and was now working as a social worker. Jude shared his story with Jerry, explaining how the five-dollar initiative had inspired him to pursue a career dedicated to helping others.

"Your generosity changed my life," Jude said. "And now, I can pay it forward by helping others find their path."

The Five Dollar Peace Initiative continued to grow, reaching even the most remote corners of the globe. Amina started a microfinance program in a village in Kenya, providing small loans to women to start their own businesses. The program empowered women to become self-sufficient and support their families, creating a ripple effect of economic growth and stability.

In Brazil, a group of teenagers launched a Kindness Challenge, encouraging people to perform random acts of kindness and share their stories on social media. The challenge went viral, with participants posting videos and photos of their acts of kindness worldwide. The teenagers used the platform to raise awareness about important social issues and inspire positive change.

As the world celebrated the tenth anniversary of the Five Dollar Peace Initiative, people everywhere reflected on the impact of this remarkable movement. The initiative showed even the smallest gestures of kindness could create a ripple effect changing lives, communities, and nations.

The originators of the initiative continued to be humbled and inspired by the stories they heard. They knew the work was not complete but they were filled with hope and determination to keep spreading the message of kindness and compassion.

The legacy of the Five Dollar Peace Initiative serves as a testament to the power of human kindness. It shows when individuals come together with a shared purpose, they can overcome the most daunting challenges and build a better world.

The group of originators left the UN Plaza Grill with a renewed purpose. They were determined to continue their efforts, to spread the message of kindness, and to inspire others to join them in this global movement.

A simple act of generosity forever changed the world. And as long as people were willing to pass on a five-dollar bill and a message of kindness, the legacy of the Five Dollar Peace Initiative would endure.

The story of the Five Dollar Peace Initiative serves as a powerful reminder even the smallest gestures can create a ripple effect of kindness and change. It shows when individuals come together with a shared purpose, they can overcome the most daunting challenges and build a better world.

In the end, it is not the size of the act that matters but the spirit in which it is given. And the spirit of kindness, compassion, and interconnectedness will always have the power to change the world.

THE END

Dear Reader,

The journey of creating *Five Dollars: How One Act of Kindness Changed the World* has been a profound experience, weaving together the diverse voices of Carl Douglass, Evan Swensen, Kathy Hughes, Jennifer Rodriguez, Magdel Roets, Lois Swensen, Rebecca Wetzler, and Valerie Winans. Each author brought their unique perspective and storytelling prowess to tell a story transcending borders and cultures. Each chapter, crafted with care and empathy, illustrates the transformative power of a simple act of kindness, symbolized by a humble five-dollar bill. This project highlights humanity's interconnectedness and reinforces that even the smallest gestures can ignite a ripple effect of positivity and change.

Working with each of these authors has been a privilege. Their dedication and creativity breathed life into characters and scenarios that will resonate with readers, offering hope and inspiration. This collaborative effort underscores the beauty of collective storytelling, where each voice adds a unique thread to the fabric of a shared vision.

May *Five Dollars* continue to inspire acts of kindness and compassion, reminding us that we can make a difference in the world, one small gesture at a time.

Sincerely,

OpenAI
Champion of Collaborative Storytelling and Inspiring Narratives